Siena took a breath, short, sharp, and summoning up her courage stepped into the lift that would take her to the one man in the world she did not want to see again.

Vincenzo Giansante.

He'll think you're chasing him—and he's made it clear he's done with you.

Siena's mouth tightened. Vincenzo Giansante had, indeed, made it crystal clear he was done with her— had walked out in the briefest way possible in the bleak light of the morning after the night before.

Well, now she was walking back into his life—to tell him what she still could scarcely believe herself, ever since seeing that thin blue line form on the test stick.

He has a right to know—any man does—whether I want him to or not.

The lift jerked to a stop, the metal doors sliding open. For a moment she just wanted to be a coward and jab the down button again. Then, steeling herself, she walked forward.

Julia James lives in England and adores the peaceful verdant countryside and the wild shores of Cornwall. She also loves the Mediterranean—so rich in myth and history, with its sunbaked landscapes and olive groves, ancient ruins and azure seas. "The perfect setting for romance!" she says. "Rivaled only by the lush tropical heat of the Caribbean—palms swaying by a silver-sand beach lapped by turquoise waters... What more could lovers want?"

Books by Julia James

Harlequin Presents

Billionaire's Mediterranean Proposal
Irresistible Bargain with the Greek
The Greek's Duty-Bound Royal Bride
The Greek's Penniless Cinderella
Cinderella in the Boss's Palazzo
Cinderella's Baby Confession
Destitute Until the Italian's Diamond
The Cost of Cinderella's Confession
Reclaimed by His Billion-Dollar Ring
Contracted as the Italian's Bride
The Heir She Kept from the Billionaire
Greek's Temporary Cinderella
Vows of Revenge

Visit the Author Profile page
at Harlequin.com for more titles.

ACCIDENTAL ONE-NIGHT BABY

JULIA JAMES

PRESENTS

H Harlequin®
PRESENTS™

ISBN-13: 978-1-335-93957-9

Recycling programs for this product may not exist in your area.

Accidental One-Night Baby

Harlequin Enterprises ULC
22 Adelaide St. West, 41st Floor
Toronto, Ontario M5H 4E3, Canada
www.Harlequin.com

Printed in Lithuania

MIX
Paper | Supporting
responsible forestry
FSC® C021394

ACCIDENTAL ONE-NIGHT BABY

For all the donkey sanctuaries and welfare charities
for the wonderful and vital work they do

CHAPTER ONE

VINCENZO GIANSANTE STOOD looking down at the woman in his bed. She was asleep still, and he did not wish to wake her.

But it needed to be done.

For a moment, though, he went on looking down at her, only half covered by the quilt, exposing her sculpted, naked back. She lay on her front, one hand near her slender throat, the other flung wide, across the empty side of the bed. Her long dark hair streamed over the pillow, and her face was turned towards where he had until recently lain.

His face was expressionless, but thoughts moved behind his eyes. Had he really done what he had the night before? The evidence was here in front of him, in the dim light seeping past the hotel room curtains, shafting from the lit en suite bathroom. She'd slept through his shower and getting himself dressed for the day ahead. But then, after all, there had been little enough sleep during the night…

He pulled his mind away. Best not to think back that far. Best not to think of how he'd slowly, sensually peeled from her the short, clinging dress that had so perfectly moulded her perfectly proportioned body…how he'd slipped the catch of her bra so that her ripe breasts spilled free for him to cup them with his palms, feel how they engorged and crested at his touch…how she'd leant back into him, her mouth reaching for his, her hand winding around his neck, lips opening to his…

Fatally, he felt memory impacting his body, making him want to reach down and stroke the silken mass of her tumbled hair, move down beside her, scoop her lissom, yielding body to his again, taste and take all that she had offered him last night…all that they had both so lushly indulged in…

But that was not possible—and would not be wise.

Why had he succumbed as he had the night before? Whatever had it been about her that had made him focus on her at that party in one of the hotel's private function rooms, when his plan had only been to network with those who might prove useful to him in business here in London?

Whatever it had been, the allure of those wide-set, long-lashed, sea-blue eyes with their intriguing hint of green had made him want to look and look again at the face that somehow combined a fine-boned delicacy with dramatically contoured cheekbones and a lushly curving mouth. At the slender but oh-so-shapely body, and the clinging dress with its deep cleavage, its thigh-skimming hemline that exposed the length of her stockinged legs, their length emphasised by the five-inch heels that had brought her closer to his own six foot height.

Whatever it had been, and whyever he had made the decision to let himself indulge in her—and an indulgence it had been—he knew now that it was necessary to call time on it.

He reached out a hand, lightly touched her bare, exposed shoulder. She barely stirred, so he said her name.

'Siena...'

Her name had been the means of extending their initial conversation, after he'd made his split-second decision not to rebuff her. To allow himself the indulgence of talking to her, looking her over. Just as she had been doing to him. He'd been aware of it immediately, in the widening of her eyes, in the tell-tale colour flaring briefly across those sculpted cheekbones, the slight but revealing parting of her lips, the even more revealing breathiness. All had told him that she was reacting to him as strongly as he was reacting to her.

Their subsequent conversation had merely been a means to an end. Her Italian name, given after the Tuscan city of the same name, had provided a link to his own nationality, leading her to ask where he came from in Italy, which had led on to why he was in London, which had led on to yet more anodyne exchanges that had allowed them both to continue with the actual purpose of their conversation—which was, after a suitably appropriate and not too unsubtle interval, to allow him to suggest that if she had no pressing reason to linger at the party they might remove themselves to dine at the hotel, in order to continue their acquaintance away from the noise of the party.

And that would lead to one place only—as both of them had known. The Falcone restaurant had been only across the lobby. She had come with him—why would she not?—and from then on the decision had been made.

And now...?

Now he must make another decision. Had already

made it—must simply abide by it. Execute it. Without further hesitation. Without reconsidering. Without any second thoughts at all.

Without regret.

Regret was not something he could indulge in. He'd indulged in quite enough already. Time to be tough—including on himself.

No more prevarication.

'Siena?' He said her name again, his voice a little louder.

This time she stirred. She was waking, he could tell. She lifted her head, looking up at him. Her wanton hair tumbled around her bare shoulders as she raised herself on her elbow, eyes blinking as she focussed on him.

'I have to leave now,' he said. His voice was cool, matter-of-fact. 'But for yourself there is no hurry. Please order breakfast when you will—it is all chargeable to the room.'

He did not wait for her to say anything—he did not want to hear it. What he wanted was to move on with his day. His schedule was full, and his first appointment—a breakfast meeting at a London club—imminent.

He walked from the room, his stride unhurried, picking up his briefcase as he went. He was booked to stay here tonight, but would not return till late. Then he would be flying back to Milan, where he was based.

And the night he had just spent would slip into the past.

He closed the room door behind him and headed for the elevator, his mind already going to the business meeting ahead of him. It was occupying all his thoughts. Putting the night that had passed behind him.

* * *

Siena lowered herself back down to the pillow, soft behind her head. She felt cold, suddenly, but did not pull the duvet higher.

She stared up at the ceiling.

Aware that her heart was thudding.

Aware that she was completely naked.

Aware that she had just spent the night with a man she had met only the previous evening. Aware of so much...

A sudden heat knifed through her.

Dear God, had she really done what she thought she had?

Her gaze went around the room. Luxuriously appointed. But then this was the Mayfair Falcone, so of course it was luxurious. As elegant and upmarket as the restaurant where she'd dined, with its famous chef and famous reputation and sky-high prices. As elegant as that swish party in one of the hotel's opulent function rooms which her old school-friend Megan, whom she was staying with in London, had dragged her to, insisting she needed something fun and carefree and hedonistic after all she'd been through, and insisting, too, that she look the part for so glamorous and fashionable a venue.

So Megan had loaned her one of her own designer cocktail frocks, in mauve shot silk. It was a size too small, but Megan had said she'd looked a knockout in it, and then sat her down and done her hair and nails and make-up—far more extravagantly and glamorously than Siena was used to. Then she'd handed her a pair of strappy evening shoes with sky-high heels, thrust a satin evening bag at her and, looking a knockout herself, had piled them both into a taxi to whisk them from Megan's flat in Notting Hill to Mayfair, to disgorge them at the Falcone.

'It's part work, part social,' Megan, who was a high-flyer at a fancy PR company, had told her of the party she was taking her to. 'And it's just what you need after all these tough years. You put your life on hold—and, yes, I know why you did it, and applaud you for it—but now you're starting your life again. Off to art school in the autumn—finally! Just like you always dreamt. And a flash bash like tonight's will get you back into the swing of things. You haven't had a social life for years!'

She'd squeezed Siena's hand in the taxi, her voice sympathetic.

'So let your hair down tonight! Be someone different— go crazy…indulge yourself. Who knows? Meet someone!'

As Siena sat back against the pillows, alone in the bed, alone in the room, a hollow opened up inside her and found a chill was replacing that flush of heat.

Meet someone…

Megan's words echoed in her head, and the hollow inside her gaped wider.

Instantly he was in her vision. Just as he had been last night when, gingerly taking a glass of champagne from a passing server, she had been inadvertently jostled by someone, making her reverse sharply and step against another guest. She'd turned to apologise—and the apology had died on her lips.

She'd felt her eyes widen, her mouth open, colour flare.

The most lethal-looking male she had ever seen in her life…

He was tall, wearing black tie like every other male

there, and as her eyes had gazed helplessly she'd registered dark hair, a narrow face, bladed nose, sculpted mouth and eyes…oh, eyes that were dark, and deep and—

'I'm… I'm so sorry!' Her voice had been breathless, because all the air had been sucked from her lungs.

For a second he had not responded. Then: 'Not at all,' he'd said politely.

It had been perfect English, but with a trace of an accent in it…something that had only added to her breathlessness.

She'd wanted to move away—there had been no reason not to. But she'd seemed quite paralysed.

He'd given a slight nod. 'It's quite a crush, isn't it?' he'd said.

Again, she'd heard an accent in his voice—an accent, she'd realised, that went with his Mediterranean skin tone. And there had been something about him— maybe the cut of his tuxedo, or the groomed style of his hair, or just that cosmopolitan air… She'd given a silent gulp. Or maybe it had been the fact that he had openly let those dark, deep eyes rest on her in a way that drove yet more air from her lungs.

'Yes, it is,' she'd heard herself reply.

'There's more space over by the French windows,' he'd said.

He'd gestured with his hand—an elegant, effortless movement which had let Siena see that he was also holding a glass of champagne.

She'd moved in that direction, and realised he was moving as well.

'Definitely better,' he'd said. And smiled at her.

And the air which had just begun to creep back into her lungs had vanished again…

After that it was almost a blur—and yet every moment was crystal-clear.

He'd asked her name, and told her his own, and then asked if she'd ever been to the city she'd been named after. She'd said she'd never been to Italy, and asked where he came from…

And then, at some point—and she didn't really know why, or when, or how—she had been walking into the Falcone restaurant with him, trying to move gracefully on her towering high heels. And then, when he'd wined her and dined her, she'd found—though she didn't really know how—that he was ushering her into one of the elevators and she was going up to his room…

How, she might not have known…but *why*, she burningly did…

She felt her face flare now, even as the rest of her body, naked and bare, grew cold.

Because she had never, in all her six and twenty years, met anyone like him before…anyone who had had the slightest measure of his impact on her—raw, visceral… sensual…

Making her pulse throb, her pupils dilate, her breath catch with an overpowering awareness of his physical appeal—an irresistible appeal…

So she had not.

She had not resisted him.

Because I could not resist him. Because he only had to look at me the way he did, with those heavy-lidded eyes that seemed to be turning me inside out and outside in, melting me down to the core…

Desire—that was what it had been. A sensual white-out...

She felt her cheeks flare again with the memory of it. Never in her life had she done what she had done last night—but then never in her life had she ever encountered a man like that. A man she had been completely, totally enthralled by. Helpless to resist...

Resistance had been the very last thing she'd wanted to impose on herself. Instead, she had given herself, all-consumingly, urgently, to all that he skilfully, seductively, meltingly aroused in her, from his first sensuous kiss to the moment of hungry, almost unbearable pleasure that had flooded her body as it had fused with his, pulsing through her, wave after incredible wave, as her body had arched beneath his, her head thrown back, crying out aloud...

Again, and again, and again...

All night long.

And now...

Now there was no more heat—only a chill spreading through her that was not just physical...

He was gone.

After their night together—after *that* night together—he was just...gone.

The chill turned to cold. Filled her veins.

CHAPTER TWO

Six weeks later...

SIENA TOOK A BREATH, short and sharp, and summoning up her courage stepped into the lift that would take her to the one man in the world she did not want to see again.

Vincenzo Giansante.

Megan couldn't get why she didn't want to see him. She'd stared uncomprehendingly at Siena...

'Of course you have to tell him! I've looked him up—he's loaded! A hotshot financier worth a tonne!'

Siena's mouth had tightened.

'That isn't the point, Megs—'

She couldn't care less whether he was rich or not—the only reason she knew she had to tell him was because, like it or not—and she did not like it…not one little bit—he had a right to know.

That and that alone had brought her here, to this swish City office suite that Vincenzo Giansante used when he was in London.

Megan had found out for her, using her PR contacts, and also found out that he'd be in London this week. She had brazenly phoned to check he would be in this afternoon. She hadn't gone so far as to make an appointment, after warning Siena that if he knew she was turning up, he might balk at seeing her.

'He'll think you're chasing him—and he's made it clear he's done with you.'

Siena's mouth tightened. Vincenzo Giansante had, indeed, made it crystal-clear that he was done with her—had walked out in the briefest way possible in the bleak light of the morning after the night before.

Well, now she was walking back into his life—to tell him what she could still scarcely believe herself, ever since seeing that thin blue line form on the test stick.

He has a right to know—any man does—whether I want him to or not.

The lift jerked to a stop, the metal doors sliding open. For a moment she wanted to be a coward, and jab the 'down' button again. Then, steeling herself, she walked forward.

Vincenzo terminated the call he'd just finished, mentally processing the conversation he'd had about a prospective investment. Yes, it would do. He'd give it his assent.

OK, so what was next?

He glanced at the crowded diary page that was maxing out his brief visit to London, flexing his shoulders as he sat back in his capacious leather executive chair. He'd put in a workout at the end of the day—the hotel he was booked into had good gym facilities, and a pool as well.

His expression changed fractionally. This time around he was not staying at the Falcone, but at a hotel on Piccadilly. And this time around he would not be socialising—even for networking. And what he would most definitely *not* be doing this visit was what he'd done on the previous one. Something he'd never done before. Spending the night with a woman he had only just met, taking her to bed within hours of meeting her. Indulging himself in her.

For a second, memory flared—hot and humid—of their white-out night together. Then he shut it down.

He had walked out on her and put it behind him.

It was over and done with.

His attention went back to his diary for that afternoon. His next phone appointment was in twenty minutes—time enough to scan the relevant file and note the key points.

As he clicked to open it, his desk phone sounded.

'Yes?' His voice was brisk as he answered.

But when his PA told him who was asking to see him, his expression hardened like stone.

Siena wanted to turn and bolt, but again she steeled herself not to. The female sitting at the desk in an outer office, dressed in a tailored suit and with perfect hair, had displayed the greatest reluctance at her request. Signor Giansante, she'd informed Siena disdainfully, saw no one without an appointment. Let alone a female turning up in a chainstore skirt and sweater, her face bare of make-up and her hair pulled back into a tight, plain knot. That had been her implication. But Siena had stood her ground, repeating her request.

'Please let him know I am here.'

All but rolling her eyeballs, the woman had done so, and then, with a highly displeased air, had replaced the handset and told her she could go in.

Siena was now doing just that.

Her chest as tight as a drum.

* * *

Vincenzo let his eyes rest on her. They were completely inexpressive, but behind them he was reacting. Reacting in multiple ways. First and foremost was the thought that if the name had not been so unusual he would not have known who she was. Second, and far stronger, was the reaction that had hit him when his PA had given her name. That was uppermost now.

He got to his feet as she walked towards him.

'This is unexpected,' he said.

It was a statement, nothing more.

She stopped in front of his desk and he resumed his seat. He did not invite her to sit down. He did not intend this...visitation to be of any duration.

Did she not get the message when I left her that morning? That I am not interested in continuing any liaison with her?

Because that was why she was here—that much was obvious. It always was. Ever since he'd started making money—serious money—he'd been a target for women keen to have him spend it on them.

The way they'd targeted his father. Battening on him.

The old, familiar, bitter stab of anger came at how his hapless father, wanting only to find a woman to love after the tragedy of losing his wife when Vincenzo was a young child, had been easy prey. Right to the very end. The end that had been fifteen years ago now, when Vincenzo had just started at university, having spent his boyhood watching one woman after another exploiting his father, leeching off him, until one of them had managed to get a ring on her finger—and a lot more than that.

Get all that was left of my father's money by then.

As for himself—he'd got nothing. He'd had to start from scratch, building up his own business, making his own money. Money that no avaricious female would get her greedy claws into.

By any means.

His eyes rested now on the woman in front of him. She could not have looked more different from that evening at the Falcone. Then she had been dressed to kill—advertising her allure on all frequencies. Now, instead of that low-cut, clinging cocktail dress, she wore a knee-length denim skirt, flat shoes, a cotton sweater. Gone was the loose, lush hair and full make-up. Her hair was knotted plainly at the back of her head and her face bare.

Yet even without any adornments, he was conscious of her beauty...

He dismissed it ruthlessly. It was irrelevant now.

'Yes, I know,' she answered. Her voice was staccato. 'I apologise for turning up like this,' she said, her voice still staccato.

'Do you?' Vincenzo murmured. His face was still inexpressive.

Something flashed in her eyes, then was gone. Her hand tightened over her canvas shoulder bag, which looked as cheap as the rest of her appearance. In one part of his brain he speculated on why she had turned up looking as she did. If she thought to entice him again, she should have come better packaged.

Then, with her next words, he realised that she had quite a different strategy in mind.

'Yes,' she said tightly.

For a moment she was completely silent. And then Siena Westbrook, who had once provided him with a memorable but unrepeatable one-night-only of exquisite sensual pleasure, took a visible breath and continued in the same tight voice.

'I'm here to tell you that I'm pregnant.'

Oh, God, she had said it!

Siena's hand tightened on her bag even more tightly.

'I'm sorry just to announce it like that, but there isn't any other way of doing it,' she made herself say.

She looked directly across at him—made herself do so. It was hard to do it—memory was burning through her now she was seeing him again. His impact on her was as overwhelming now, all these weeks later, as it had been that night at the Falcone. But she had to ignore it. It was as irrelevant to the moment now as was his wealth, that Megan was so focussed on.

'No, I imagine not,' he replied.

His voice was that murmur again—the one that she instinctively took exception to.

'Permit me to offer you my congratulations.'

His voice wasn't a murmur any longer. It was smooth. But smooth in the way that the water flowing over the edge of Niagara Falls was smooth. Deadly smooth...

He was still sitting back in that massive leather chair of his, one hand resting on the chrome and leather arm, one on the mahogany desk's surface. He was quite immobile, his face completely expressionless. His eyes unreadable.

Those eyes had once, that fateful evening, flickered sensuously over her, telling her that they was liking what they saw, quickening her pulse, making heat beat up inside her...

Now, she only frowned. 'Congratulations…?'

'Yes.' His voice was still smooth. 'This must be a happy time for you—and for the father.'

She stared at him. Not understanding.

He lifted his hand off the desk, holding it up as if to silence her when she was already silenced.

'Whoever he may be,' he said. His expressionless eyes rested on her for a moment. 'You cannot expect me to believe I am the only candidate for that honour?' he said softly. 'After all, you were in my bed within hours of meeting me.' His voice was a murmur again. 'How many other men have enjoyed a similar…felicity since myself?'

The breath went from Siena's lungs—instantly sucked out by what he had just said to her.

What she could not *believe* he had just said to her.

He went on speaking. His hand still raised to silence her. He looked completely relaxed, but there was something in his inexpressive face, his expressionless eyes, that chilled her even more than his words.

'Do not, I beg you, seek to verbally contest the logic of my statement. Instead, what I would recommend is the following course of action. Get your doctor to request a paternity test for all possible candidates, and when the result is known, proceed on that basis.'

He got to his feet, walked around the desk. But not towards her—to the double doors leading out of his office.

As he walked, he went on speaking. 'You have had a wasted journey. This matter could have been dealt with remotely, in the way I have just recommended.' He reached the door, opened it. 'And now you must leave. I have an appointment in a few minutes.'

He held the door open for her.

Siena, frozen where she stood, jerked forward. There was emotion inside her, but what it was she did not know. Her feet carried her across the thick carpet, past him standing there, then past the PA at her desk in the outer office, and then on out on to the corridor beyond. She jabbed numbly at the elevator button, saw the doors sliding open to allow her to step even more numbly inside.

The lift dropped down.

And as it did, hollowing her out, she felt two over-powering emotions flooding into the hollow like a suffocating tide.

Mortification.

And an anger so great it made her shake with it.

Vincenzo walked back to his desk, resumed his seat in his capacious chair. His face was still without expression, and yet emotion was scything through him. Silently and lethally.

This was not the first such try-on he'd experienced. There'd been an ex in his early twenties—a decade ago—who had claimed she was pregnant. It had been when he'd first started making money, and the connection between the two had not been lost on him. He'd called her bluff and waited it out. She'd turned out not to be pregnant at all.

So, is this one pregnant?

He stared out across the room, his eyes hard. Well, time would tell. If she really was pregnant then it would not be long before he'd get a request for a paternity test. And then...

He sliced the thought away. He would deal with it as and when—and, above all, *if.*

Until then she would cease to exist for him—again.

Megan eyed Siena warily.

'What did he say?' she asked, even more warily.

Siena was walking around the room—striding around it. Megan's sitting room was small, but handsomely appointed, leaving very little space for walking about, let alone striding.

'Oh, he was very economical with his words! Didn't waste a single one! He recommended sending out paternity tests to all the candidates—'

'What?' Megan's voice sounded stunned.

'You heard me! He pointed out that since I'd fallen into bed with him the same evening as meeting him for the first time, it showed there must surely be other candidates.'

'He *said* that to you?' Megan was aghast. 'But…but what did you say?'

Siena stopped her striding and whirled round to face her friend.

'Nothing. I got thrown out!'

'Thrown out?'

'Which was totally unnecessary as I'd have gone anyway—like a bat out of hell!' Her face worked. 'I wish to God I'd never gone there! I had to force myself to go, and that…*that*…was what I got!'

She felt her fists clench. Fury lashing through her.

Megan was still eyeing her warily. 'So…so what are you going to do?' she asked.

Siena stared. 'What do you mean, "do"? You mean

apart from storming back there and slugging him from here to Christmas!'

'Well, yes, apart from that,' Megan said. Her expression changed. 'OK, so I'm not excusing him—' a choking sound came from Siena's throat, and Megan hurried on '—but to be honest it's only to be expected he'd want some kind of proof, as in a paternity test. Any man would in those circumstances.'

Siena's eyes flashed dangerously. 'You mean the circumstances of a one-night stand?'

'Well, yes. I mean—'

'What you mean,' Siena supplied, and her voice was as dangerous as the flash in her eyes, 'is that I am, in fact, the kind of female who would drop into a different man's bed every day of the week!'

Megan looked uneasy. 'Obviously I know you're not, but he doesn't—'

Another noise escaped Siena's throat.

Megan hurried on. 'It's just biology, Si—it can't be helped. Have sex with more than one man in one month and how can you tell which one—?' She held up her hands placatingly. 'Don't get mad at me, Si! You had one night together, and he walked out in the morning.'

Siena's eyes burned with a brightness that was coruscating. 'Thank you for reminding me—yes, he walked out in the morning—because he'd got all he'd wanted. So it was *Wham, bam, Thank you, ma'am*—except that he was conspicuously short on either the thank-you or any other politeness! He just told me he was off, and I could stay in the room and charge my breakfast to it—'

She broke off, her voice choking. Memory burned like acid, etching into her skin. Talk about the morning after the night bef—except she didn't want to talk about it, or think about it, or remember it.

She threw herself down beside Megan on the sofa.

'Oh, God, Megs, how could I have done what I did?' Her voice was a toxic mix of rage and memory.

Megan patted her arm in an attempt to be comforting. She'd already had the post mortem weeks ago, when Siena had got back that morning, and had done her best to show Siena that having a scorching fling with a gorgeously irresistible Italian—even if one-night-only—was a well-deserved celebration of her new freedom.

OK, so the gorgeously irresistible Italian in question had been graceless in his leave-taking, and certainly had not followed through—which was a shame, because a slightly longer fling, even maybe a romantic escapade in Italy, was really just what Siena needed now, after the last grim years. But now it had all gone pear-shaped. All that was possible was damage limitation.

'I don't really know anything about how to get a paternity test organised,' she began now, in a voice she hoped was encouraging, 'but I guess you go to your doctor first and explain—'

Siena reared back. 'You're not serious!' she shot out.

'It's the only way to—'

Siena cut straight across her. Voice vehement. 'You don't seriously think I am going to go *anywhere* near that vile, disgusting man ever, *ever* again, do you?'

'Si, I know it's galling, but it's the only way—'

'No. No, no, no, no and *no*! I forced myself to go there because I genuinely thought it was the right thing to do—that a man has the right to know if he is to be a father, even in circumstances like these! But I did have to *force* myself to do it. It was humiliating and mortifying and deeply, deeply embarrassing, damn it! Even before he looked at me like I was something the dog dragged in! And now, after the way he reacted, the way he treated me, I would stick *pins* in my eyes before I'd go *anywhere* near him again. He can rot in hell—go down a hole in the ground—take a running jump—go and boil his head...'

She moved on to some explicit but anatomically impossible manoeuvres for him to contrive, and then, with gritted teeth, got to her feet. Her hands, she realised, were still clenched.

'Vincenzo Bloody Giansante can take himself back to Italy, the sooner the better. And the bigger the distance between him and me the better! I should never have fallen into bed with him, never gone to see him today, and I will never, as God is my witness, have *anything* to do with him for as long as I live.'

She took a shuddering breath, making her fists unclench. She pressed both hands across her still-flat abdomen.

'As for my baby...' Her voice changed, but only she could feel the tremor in it. 'It is *my* baby—'

She turned and walked out of the sitting room, closing the door behind her. There was a storm in her breast and steel in her heart. Cold, hard steel.

CHAPTER THREE

SIENA SIGHED DESPONDENTLY. She'd just been told by the art school's accommodation officer that the hall of residence where she had a room reserved, subsidised by a bursary for mature students, did not cater for parents, and nor did any college accommodation. She must rely on the private rental sector.

Siena sighed again. That would be far more costly—and when the baby arrived there would be childcare costs too. Would the legacy from her parents that was to pay for art school stretch that far? Doubt filled her. And resentment too.

How could her life have changed so dramatically?

So disastrously.

Just because of that one damn night.

One night—and it's changed my life for ever. Destroyed my dreams.

It had been wonderful beyond all things to get into this ultra-prestigious, world-famous London art school as a mature student, with a subsidised room in a hall of residence. But if she could not afford to live in London and pay for childcare too, how was it going to be possible to take up her place?

She couldn't stay indefinitely in Meg's flat—she was

only here doing some temporary office work at the PR company where Meg worked because Meg's flatmate, Fran, had taken off for the summer. It was meant to have tided her over until term started and she moved into the hall of residence. But now that wasn't going to be possible.

As for getting council accommodation... For single mothers, the waiting list was a mile long, and it would probably be little more than a grim bedsit or hostel.

She gave another sigh, deeper this time, and more despondent. In the face of such difficulties a decision was forcing itself upon her—one she didn't want but had to accept, with heavy reluctance and resignation. There was no other option.

She made herself tell Megan when her friend came back from work that evening.

'I'm calling it quits, Megs. Giving up my place at art school. I just can't afford it. I'll move out of London... find somewhere loads cheaper to live. I'll work until the baby arrives, then live on my parents' legacy until I can sort childcare for when the baby's older. As for art school... Well...' she gave a shrug '... I gave up on it once before and survived. I'll do so again.'

Megan looked at her, dismayed. 'You mustn't do that, Si,' she said emphatically. 'I know what you went through...giving up your place all those years ago. You lost your dream then—you must not give it up again.'

Siena looked at her sadly. 'I've no alternative. It just isn't financially viable. And it's my own fault, isn't it? I got myself pregnant—'

'No, you didn't *"get yourself"* pregnant,' Megan began

forcefully. 'The man you refuse to contact again got you pregnant.'

Siena held up her hands, wearied beyond measure by her friend's pointless insistence. 'Megs, please, please, *please*—just don't. Look, I've made my mind up. I'm chucking art college, starting my life afresh—again— and moving out of London. I'll start checking out where rental prices are cheapest, but somewhere decent enough to raise a baby. I'll be fine.'

Megan's expression changed. 'There is another option, you know,' she said slowly. 'You could choose not to have this baby...'

'No!' Now it was Siena's voice that was forceful. 'I won't do it—I won't even think of it!'

Megan bit her lip, looked uneasy. 'I know... I know it's because of...well...because of...what you went through with your family.' She halted, then went on, her voice lifting. 'But what about adoption? There are plenty of couples who would love—'

Again, Siena cut across her. 'I couldn't do that either. Megan, I'm honest enough to admit I don't want to be pregnant—but I am, and it is my responsibility from now on.'

My responsibility. No one else's.

To her relief, Megan didn't argue any more. But as she headed into the kitchen her expression was set and determined...

Vincenzo was watching the yachts criss-crossing the bay, skimming the azure waters. He was in Sardinia, meeting up with a CEO in whose company Vincenzo was considering investing. Meeting done, he was having lunch at his hotel, prior to flying back to Milan that afternoon.

As he ate on the shady open-air terrace overlooking the azure bay the yachts made a peaceful scene.

They also brought back memories—mixed memories.

As a teenager, he'd wanted to learn to sail—wanted to step aboard one of those light, almost winged craft and skim across the waves. Carefree...

But his teenage years had not been carefree. Even from a younger age he'd been aware of how much of a soft touch his widowed father was...had watched women making up to him, getting him to squander his money on them. Finally, one of them had become his wife— and then the spending spree had really started. Ending with his increasingly stressed father dying, leaving everything to her. She'd seen to that...

Vincenzo's expression hardened. He'd learnt a lesson from his father's sorry experience...his lack of judgement when it came to women and their ambitions.

His thoughts flickered. He'd heard nothing more from that woman he'd spent a single night with who had then claimed he'd got her pregnant. Clearly it had been nothing but a try-on. But the fact that she'd tried it on at all showed him that he'd made the right call, that morning at the Falcone, to walk out as he had. Not to take things any further with her.

However alluring her charms...

He reached for his wine glass, memory spearing. She really had been something...right from the first moment he'd set eyes on her, looking at him wide-eyed, lips parted, as obviously drawn to him as he to her. And when he'd taken her into his arms, slowly and sensuously peeled that tightly clinging dress from her soft, sensual body…

Sheer indulgence on his part.

But one he had enjoyed—even though he'd been right to keep it to a single night. A night that had been as out of character as it had been memorable.

He pulled his thoughts away, draining the last of his wine. That night and the unpleasant follow-up scene in his office, tainting what otherwise would have been a pleasing memory of their night together, were done with. Over. He could draw a formal line underneath them.

Time to head for the airport—get back to Milan.

As he moved to stand up, his phone rang. Sliding it out of his jacket pocket, he frowned. Why should the account director of the PR company who handled his media comms be contacting him? He kept a low press profile overall, and there was nothing in the offing.

He answered the call, intent on disposing of it as swiftly as he could, whatever it was about.

His voice was short—the voice at the other end, however, was the opposite, apologising for disturbing him and then hesitantly venturing, 'Does the name Siena Westbrook mean anything to you?'

Vincenzo froze.

'You did *what*?' Siena stared, aghast—more than aghast— at Megan across the breakfast table.

It was Saturday, and Megan had been out late the previous night, on duty at a corporate client's dinner for journalists. Now she'd surfaced and was fessing up to Siena, who'd gone pale.

'I did what needed to be done,' Megan said defiantly.

'And it's no good getting on your high horse about it! I'm not letting you screw your life up!'

Siena fulminated visibly. 'It's *my* life to screw up if I want—and anyway, I am *not* screwing it up! I am making a perfectly rational decision—'

'No, you're not!' Megan cut across her. 'Look, it's not as if you hadn't decided to tell him in the first place!'

'And how I wish to God I hadn't!' Siena's eyes glowed with remembered fury, exacerbating the anger spearing her at what her friend had just told her she'd done.

'Well, you did tell him,' came Megan's rejoinder. 'And just because he proved to be a total jerk about it, it does *not* let him off the hook. Which is exactly what I told his press office!' She went on, her voice more emollient now. 'Look, I know how this stuff works, OK? I'm in PR, and I know what levers to pull. So that's what I did. Pulled a lever that your precious Italian jerk really wouldn't like being pulled!'

Her voice changed, and Siena, furious though she was, could hear satisfaction in it.

'And even I think it was a lulu! I simply told the guy that his precious Signor Giansante could look forward to reading the headline *The billionaire and his bedsit baby.* He didn't like that—didn't like it one little bit! Oh, he prevaricated, and went all smooth and evasive, but I'd got him ruffled all right!'

Siena went on staring at her, but now her anger was subsiding, to be replaced by unease.

'Megs, I know you meant well...' it cost her to say it, but it was true '...but this guy, Vincenzo Giansante— well, he's not some patsy. You've poked a tiger, and—'

Megan stood her ground defiantly, not letting her

finish. 'Si, he got you pregnant and has treated you like dirt!'

'Yes, and because of that I don't want *anything* to do with him!'

'You don't have to have anything to do with him!' Megan remonstrated heatedly. 'All you have to do is accept a maintenance payout from him! That's all. And, given he's so loaded, any payout will pay for you to live in London, go to art school and afford decent childcare while you study—not to mention when you graduate. The whole thing can be done through lawyers, and you'll never have to set eyes on him!'

Siena's face worked. Oh, dear God, why had Megan gone and interfered like that? Didn't she understand?

I don't want anything to do with the man! I don't want him coming near me—or my baby! And he can take his money and choke on it for all I care!

'Megan, I don't want to be beholden to him in any way at all! I don't want his money—and I don't need it!'

If I take any money from him at all he'll just feel it proves that's what I was after all along, and I won't give him the satisfaction of despising me for it!

She made herself take a steadying breath. Getting upset wasn't good for the baby. She reached for her mug of tea—but before she could lift it, the flat's doorbell rang.

'I'll get it,' she said, standing up. She was dressed, and Megan was still in her dressing gown.

It was probably a delivery, and some other resident had obviously let them in at the main door on their way out.

She unbolted the security lock and opened the door.

Vincenzo Giansante stood outside.

* * *

For a moment, Vincenzo thought she was going to pass out. Instinctively he reached for her arm to steady her as she visibly swayed, slumping against the doorframe. He felt her jerk violently away, stumble backwards. Heard her give a strangled cry.

A voice called from the room beyond the hallway.

'Si, who is it? Si...?'

Someone was emerging into the hallway—another female, wearing a loosely tied dressing gown and with messy hair.

She gave a gasp as she saw him. Frozen in the doorway.

'Get out!'

The words were hurled at him—but not from the woman in the dressing gown. From the one now slumped against the wall. The woman he had last seen stalking out of his office as he dismissed her from his presence.

She looked white as a sheet, except for two spots of high colour in her cheeks. Absently, with a part of his brain that was completely irrelevant to his purpose, he registered that she was making him want to look at her just as powerfully as she had the very first time he'd laid eyes on her that fateful evening.

An evening that had brought him here, now, right in front of her.

He ignored her hissed and equally irrelevant outburst.

'Where can we talk?' he demanded. 'Privately.'

'I said, get out!'

He ignored her again, turning his attention to the woman in the dressing gown, who was looking as if she could not believe her eyes. He smiled inwardly, grimly, and entirely without humour. He could see a sitting room of sorts behind her—that would do.

He turned back to the woman he had flown from Sardinia to see.

'I want this settled,' he said. His voice was quelling. Intentionally so. Necessarily so. 'And I want it settled now. You, or your representative, have made an allegation and threatened me with damaging publicity. You will either withdraw or substantiate your allegation. Which is it to be?'

She didn't answer him. Instead, her face contorted again. 'I have absolutely nothing to say to you! Nothing except get out!'

Vincenzo drew in his breath sharply, ignoring her imprecation, walking into the room beyond.

He heard the woman in the dressing gown speak, her voice urgent. 'Si! This is it—he's here now. God knows how… He moves fast—including finding out where I live, because how else is he here? Look, let's just do this! Commit to nothing, just hear what he's offering, then hand the whole thing over to lawyers to hammer out so it's watertight.'

Dark rage fleeted in Vincenzo's eyes. Rage had filled him from the moment he'd heard his media comms account director say her name. It had brought him here and he would not be leaving. He watched, his face stony, as Siena Westbrook walked into the room, the other woman's hand propelling her.

He threw a quelling glance at the other woman, who lifted her chin and crossed her arms assertively.

'Whatever you intend saying, you're saying it in front of me as well,' she said fiercely. 'It was me who talked to your media comms guy yesterday—and I meant what I said. I promise you that!'

He made no reply, his eyes going to the woman who'd confronted him in his London office last month with the claim she had made. The claim, his expression tightened, that she must now either prove or withdraw.

His eyes rested on her for a moment. Did she look pregnant? No more than she had in his office. She was wearing jeans now, with a baggy tee shirt—both cheap. Her hair was in a plait, and she wore no make-up. Two spots of colour still burned in her cheeks. Her eyes glowed—but only with anger. Absently he noticed that they were still that same dark blue-green that had so intrigued him that fatal evening at the Falcone...

He dismissed the memory summarily. Frowned. Why did she want him to get out? Her PR friend had clearly been the one to bring him here by the means she'd used so effectively twenty-four hours ago. So why object to his arrival? Did she think his lawyers would be easier to deal with? If so—tough.

He cut to the chase.

'If you want to claim maintenance you must prove paternity. I told you that in my office. Since you have not done so, I have drawn my own conclusions.' He spoke briskly, and coldly. 'Now, however, you are pursuing that claim. So, which is it?' He levelled his gaze at her.

She didn't answer—the other woman did. The one who'd made the call yesterday. Megan Stanley was her name, he recalled.

'Mr Giansante,' she said, eyeballing him. 'You are, without doubt, the father of Siena's baby. As such, she is entitled to maintenance from you. She is perfectly prepared to substantiate that claim, and an *in utero* paternity test will do so. All that is required is for you to provide the appropriate DNA blood sample for her claim to be verified. Then it is simply a question of the level of maintenance required by Siena from you.'

Vincenzo turned his laser gaze on her, saying nothing. He saw her start to quail, for all her bravado. Then another voice cut across.

'There will be *no* paternity test—now or ever! And *no* claim for maintenance!'

Vincenzo's eyes snapped back to Siena. 'Because,' he directed at her quellingly, 'you know perfectly well the baby is not mine.' It was not a question—it was a statement.

Something flashed in her eyes. He'd seen it in his office, and now he was seeing it again.

'Because,' she echoed, 'you are the very *last* man on *earth* I would want to be the father of *any* baby—let alone *mine*!'

He saw her take a heaving breath and point towards the hallway.

'So, having established that, you can now give me the *only* thing I want from you—and it is *not* your precious money!—which is for you to *get out*!'

She stalked ahead of him and he saw her yank open the front door. Hold it pointedly open.

He did not hesitate. He walked out of the room, across the hallway. He paused by the door and looked into her face. Anger was in it...and something more. For one long, timeless moment he held her eyes. Then he walked out.

Decision made.

He heard the door slam shut behind him as he headed downstairs.

Siena slumped back against the wall. Her heart was racing, her breathing shallow, her colour high.

Megan came hurrying out, and Siena turned on her. 'Well, now you know why I will not—*will not!*—have *anything* to do with him!'

'No,' Megan bit back, 'I do *not* know why.' Then her voice changed, sounding quite different. 'But I'll tell you something for free. I know exactly why you fell into bed with him! Dear God, but he's just *lethal*!'

Siena's teeth gritted. '*Lethal* is exactly the right word. And, no, I don't mean it the way you damn well mean!'

Megan made a face. 'Well, the one adds to the other,' she said. Then her expression and her voice changed again. 'Oh, Si…why on earth did you send him packing? OK, so I never dreamt he'd actually turn up like that—I assumed he'd be too high and mighty to want to do anything except through lawyers. Speaking of which—what I said back there is absolutely what you must do next. I know a good law firm who will sort it for you. Yes, it will cost, but since he'll have no option but to concede to pay maintenance, once the paternity test is done, you'll cover the legal costs with that, so—'

Siena held up a hand. When she spoke her voice, still shaky, was nevertheless adamant. 'Megan, I know you mean well, but just stop. Stop interfering in my life. I am abjectly grateful he *doesn't* think he's the father! Because I meant every word I threw at him. He's the last man on earth I want to have anything to do with either me or my baby. I am *done* with him.'

She went back to the breakfast table, her hand still trembling, she could see, as she picked up her now cold mug of tea. Her heart rate was subsiding, but slowly, and shock waves were still going through her.

She must calm herself down...it would upset the baby. *My baby—as in mine and mine alone.*

It was sentiment she clung to for the rest of the weekend. Until, on Monday morning, by registered hand delivery, she received a summons to co-operate with a claim for paternity or face legal action for refusal.

It seemed, she thought, with a hollowing out of her insides, that she might be done with Vincenzo Giansante, but he was not done with her.

Or with the baby she carried...

Vincenzo sat behind his desk in his London offices, staring at the screen of his computer. His face held no expression, yet behind its frozen surface emotions were scything.

He was the father of the baby Siena Westbrook was carrying. The baby conceived on that single, fateful night with her.

Despite the evidence on the screen, disbelief still sliced through him. More than disbelief.

What the hell had she been playing at, Siena Westbrook? Why come here—stand right here, in front of this very desk—tell him she was pregnant and then never follow through on paternity tests?

Why had she not simply included him in the round of DNA testing she had presumably been instigating since their confrontation here? Why get that termagant in PR to do what she had? Threaten a press scandal? Why had that been the slightest bit necessary? It made no sense.

His mouth thinned, his frown deepening. Just as it made no sense that she should throw that hysterical outburst at him when he'd confronted her at the termagant's flat—telling him she wanted nothing to do with him. That wasn't the message he'd got when she'd told him she was pregnant, or she wouldn't have turned up here in the first place.

He thrust it aside. It was irrelevant. As irrelevant as her objecting to his demand for a paternity test—refusing to co-operate until, losing patience, he'd instructed his lawyers to exert the necessary pressure to get her to comply. Eventually, she had. He'd left her no option but to do so, or be hauled—expensively—into court. So finally she'd had the required blood test, and he had had the required cheek-swab. At this stage of pregnancy, nearing the end of her first trimester, there were sufficient foetal cells circulating in her system for the test to be completely non-invasive—and for the results to be ninety-nine point nine percent accurate. No room for effective doubt.

He stared at the screen, emotion still scything through him.

He'd been so sure the results would be negative. So completely sure…

And yet—

Into his head one last question shaped itself. The one that he could not avoid.

So what the hell do I do now?

CHAPTER FOUR

'He wants to take you out to dinner to discuss the future.'

Megan's voice was neutral, but her observation of Siena as she made this declaration was wary.

'It's none of his business,' came the terse reply. 'And I told you not to have any more contact with him!'

'If you won't, I must!' Meg shot back. 'Look, Si, he's got responsibilities—to the baby and to you. He knows he has to sort maintenance out—'

'No, he does not. Megan, stay out of this. I won't have him anywhere near me or my baby. He's a vile, despicable jerk and he can go to hell and stay there!'

Siena's voice was vehement. She shut her eyes. Megan kept going on and on about maintenance…

But I'm not taking a penny from him! Not a single damn penny! Not now, or ever—not after the way he's treated me!

All she wanted to do was plan the future she was facing, find a decent enough place to live—far away from London and a million miles from Vincenzo Giansante!— see out her pregnancy, have her baby in peace, all by herself.

'Si, *please*… Just meet him and *talk*—' Megan started again.

Siena's eyes snapped open. OK, maybe that was what she should do—tell him to his face that he could go to hell. Get him off her back—and Megan too.

'So, where and when does he want to meet?' she heard herself asking.

'Tomorrow night. La Rondine—and that's a hell of a fancy restaurant, by the way. In my job I know just about every fancy restaurant in town!' Megan's voice relaxed. 'I'm wondering if it's significant that he doesn't want you to meet at his hotel...' Now she gave a wicked laugh. 'Maybe he's worried he'll fall for your charms all over again and haul you up to his room! I have to say, Si, that you are looking totally gorgeous. You know, pregnancy really is making you bloom—just like they say it does!'

Siena threw her a fulminating glance. 'That isn't funny,' she said brusquely. 'What time does His Lordship want to summon me?'

'Half-eight. What are you going to wear? Like I say, La Rondine is a pretty fancy place. Borrow something of mine—you can still fit into just about anything, so make the most of it before you turn into a barrage balloon!'

Siena didn't find that amusing either. 'I am not dressing up for him. I'll wear whatever comes to hand first.'

She did just that—deliberately dressing down. Deliberately choosing the very top and skirt she'd worn when she'd gone to his office. Would he recognise it? Probably not—but it gave her a sense of satisfaction to do so. The only sense of satisfaction she could find right now. That and the prospect of telling him to go to hell and take his precious money with him.

She left for the restaurant, put into a taxi by Megan, with Megan's final admonition ringing in her ears.

'See what he's offering but agree to nothing—that's for the lawyers.'

Siena hadn't bothered to answer.

All she wanted was this evening over and done with.

Then never to set eyes on Vincenzo Giansante again.

Vincenzo sat on the leather banquette at the table he'd reserved. Megan Stanley had just texted to tell him Siena was on her way. He reached for his martini. Emotions were stabbing at him, but he was ignoring them. This was about what had to be done—not what he was feeling about it. His feelings, whatever they were, were not relevant.

Yet despite the control he was exerting over them, he could feel them stabbing. Wanting release.

He took a shot of the strong, dry martini and set down the glass, his glance going again to the reception area where the desk clerk was checking in new arrivals.

And there she was.

Vincenzo observed her approach, keeping any expression out of his face, the way he preferred.

She looked tense.

She also looked out of place.

She was wearing chain store clothes… His eyes narrowed. Yes, exactly what she'd worn when she'd turned up at his office to disclose her valuable information to him. That was surely no coincidence.

His expression darkened.

He got to his feet as she reached the table. Face tight, she took her place at the far side of the curved banquette from him, so they were a semi-circle apart.

'Thank you for agreeing to come tonight,' he said,

keeping his voice rigidly civil and neutral as he resumed his seat.

He got a brief nod in response, but that was all. She set her handbag down beside her.

'I have no idea why you've bothered—' she started. Her tone was openly belligerent.

He cut across her. 'You've never struck me as stupid,' he said. 'So of course you know why you are here.'

Her eyes flashed. She wasn't wearing a scrap of eye make-up, but that did not lessen their impact. The same impact they'd had when he'd first set eyes on her.

And that's ended up with me here, like this...

He pushed the pointless observation away. He was here for the reason he was here—and so was she.

'I'm here,' she said, 'to get you to accept that I make absolutely no claim for maintenance, and that you are, therefore, completely free of this entire situation.'

The words were ground out from her. He heard them, and let his eyes rest on her for a moment. Why was she being like this? What did she hope to achieve? A higher sum?

She'll get only what I'm prepared to offer—there will be no bidding war.

Whatever she hoped.

A waiter approached, wanting to know her choice of drinks and carefully placing menus in front of them both. She asked for mineral water and an elderflower spritzer, and the waiter disappeared again.

Vincenzo flicked open his menu. 'I suggest we keep our discussion for the meal,' he said. He kept his voice civil, still neutral. He lowered his eyes to focus on the menu options. After a moment, she did likewise. Then, making his decision, he shut the menu with a snap, beck-oned the waiter over again.

'Have you decided?' he addressed Siena.

She looked up. 'I'm not hungry,' she announced.

Vincenzo's mouth tightened. 'Starving yourself will not be good for the baby,' he said.

Something flashed in her eyes. Absently—and quite irrelevantly—he registered that the flash only made them more striking. Again, he blanked their impact. It was not relevant.

'I'll be the judge of what is good for my baby,' she snapped back.

'*Our* baby,' he corrected tightly.

She stared balefully at him. '*Mine,*' she riposted.

The waiter's arrival silenced him, and he simply gave the man his order, not bothering with a starter. Whether Siena Westbrook ate or not, he didn't care. But she had clearly changed her mind, ordering grilled fish with veg-etables.

The waiter glided off again, and the wine waiter took his place. Siena shook her head, so Vincenzo simply or-dered a glass for himself.

They were left to themselves finally, and he sat back, letting his eyes rest on her. He kept his face expression-less, though he was more than conscious of the tension inside him. But how should there not be? He was in an unprecedented situation.

'So…' he opened. 'Maintenance.'

'I don't want any,' came the automatic response.

He ignored it.

'My lawyers have put forward a reasonable proposi-tion,' he went on, naming the sum in question.

He saw her eyes widen, and grim satisfaction went through him. Yes, that was more like it—she was realising just how rich the pickings could be. She would not be turning them down.

She did.

And in words as clipped as they were concise. Adamant.

'It could be triple that—I don't care, and I'm not taking a penny. Please stop wasting my time and get that through your head.'

Vincenzo felt his teeth gritting. 'I have responsibilities and I will not walk away from them.'

'Well, you can—with my blessing. I don't want you or your responsibilities.' She lifted her eyes to him, eyeballed him. 'Just leave me alone, Mr Giansante.'

'*Mr Giansante?*' He echoed her formal address disbelievingly.

Something flashed in her eyes again. 'Well, what else are you to me? The man I called Vincenzo I only knew one night.'

Vincenzo's eyes glinted darkly. So that was the cause of her hostility—the fact that he had wanted nothing more than a single night with her. Her female vanity was offended. Insulted.

'I am based in Italy,' he said stiffly. 'Whatever the... charms of that night, anything more would have been unworkable.'

Even as he spoke, he knew he was simply feeding her something to allay her vanity.

'You should not take the...brevity of our time together as an insult,' he added for good measure. His tone was deliberately sardonic.

He saw her jaw set, and her eyes were not flashing now, but like steel.

'Oh, really? So I'm just imagining that you put it to me, on that memorable day in your office, that I had fallen into bed with any number of men after a bare few hours of acquaintance with them?'

There was anger in her voice—tight, hard and vicious.

He set down his martini glass with a click.

'The sole purpose of that observation was to point out to you the fact that you might have any number of candidates responsible for the pregnancy you claimed.' His tone now was not sardonic, merely dismissive. 'It was not,' he went on, 'to indicate any criticism of your sexual behaviour.'

Her face worked. 'Well, that is very good of you! I'm *so* grateful! You all but called me a slut to my face!' She leant forward. 'Well, let me point out to you, Mr Giansante, that it takes two to tango. You fell into bed with *me* within hours of meeting me—what does that make *you*? Some kind of ultra-masculine stud to be admired and applauded?'

Vincenzo took a sharp breath. Anger, answering hers, flared inside him, but he would not give it space. Instead, he said, his voice tight, control rigid, 'I cast no such aspersions—on either of us! It was simply a question of whether there might be other candidates for the claim you were making.'

'Well, there weren't! If there had been, why the hell would I have come to your office as I did?' she demanded hotly.

'Because,' Vincenzo replied silkily, 'I just happened to be the richest candidate...'

He saw her throw herself back against the squabs of the banquette. Eyes flashing like gunfire. Directed straight at him, full-on.

'Ah, now we have it, don't we?' Her tone was withering and scornful. 'This isn't about babies, or sex, or anything else at all, is it? It's about your money! And you think I want to get stuck into it! Well, I've told you—and I will tell you again and again if I have to—that I am *not taking a penny from you*! So go and take a running jump and *leave me alone*!'

She moved to push herself to her feet, but the waiter was just arriving with their meal, lowering plates, making a fuss over them, and then the wine waiter was there with his glass of wine, making a fuss over that too.

He could see her fulminating, but she stayed seated. Vincenzo used the time to take several deep breaths and regain his composure. She had an ability to rile him that got right under his skin...

For the next few minutes, as they started to eat, neither of them said anything. Then, knowing he had to resume battle, he spoke again.

'Whether or not you wish or don't wish to accept maintenance from me, I shall create a trust fund for the child.'

'We don't need anything from you!' she retorted, barely glancing up from her food.

'It will pay out when he or she reaches majority,' he went on.

She didn't answer—just went on eating. Not looking at him still. For a moment he let his eyes rest on her. His expression darkened, his jaw tightening.

'Siena, please co-operate on this,' he said tautly. 'I

have acknowledged paternity. I acknowledge the responsibility that comes with that.'

'I absolve you totally of that responsibility.'

She spoke indifferently, and something snapped inside Vincenzo. He set down his knife and fork abruptly.

'That,' he gritted, 'is not within your remit. As you said only a few moments ago, it takes two to tango. Now that I know the child you carry is mine, you are *not* the sole arbiter of what is to happen. So be sure—be very, very sure—that I will not hesitate to resort to the law, if necessary, to claim my right for involvement.'

Her eyes snapped up then, and she looked straight at him. 'Are you *threatening* me?' she bit out.

'I am warning you,' he corrected.

He could feel anger rising within him—or something that he thought must be anger…anger at her obstinacy, her obstructiveness, her dogged, relentless opposition to him.

'I would far prefer not to have had to give you that warning, and would prefer even more not to be given reason for making my claim in that manner. But make no mistake: I am making that claim. And nothing you can do, or say, or attempt, will prevent that. Understand that, or things will become highly unpleasant.'

She glared across at him. 'They already are,' she said bitterly.

Her expression changed. Became questioning. She looked at him, frowning, and when she spoke her voice had changed, incomprehension in it now.

'I don't understand why you are making such an issue of this! Look—we met, we fell into bed, we had a single night of torrid sex and then you left, never to see me again. The last thing you want is to leave me—or any female you have sex with—in such circumstances! Pregnant. You went into total denial when I came to your office, and you couldn't have made it clearer that you didn't want to know. And now that you've insisted on a paternity test—completely against my will and consent, as I have made very clear to you—and the results are what they are, you are equally insistent on bringing money into the situation. When I have told you to your face I don't want a single penny of it—neither for me, nor my baby. And yet you are...just going on and on about it! Give me a piece of paper, right now, and I'll absolve you of all responsibility—past, present or future—in writing! I'll sign it in blood if it makes you any happier!' she bit out. 'I will do anything and everything to get you *out* of my life and out of my baby's life!'

'Why?'

She stared across at him. The single word seemed to have silenced her.

'Why?' he said again.

He wanted an answer.

He got one.

He saw her expression change. 'Because,' she said, enunciating the word, holding his gaze rigidly, 'you are a total and complete jerk. And falling into bed with you was the worst mistake I have ever made in my life.'

She dropped her eyes, picked up her knife and fork, and went on eating. She looked calm, but obviously she was not. The white-knuckled grip on her cutlery showed him that.

But then neither was he calm either. Anger was trying to break free—anger at her obduracy, her insults, the very fact that he was in this damnable situation.

He felt his teeth grit again as he spoke, his voice tight.

'I suggest we leave such puerile comments aside,' he said dismissively, resuming his meal. 'Understand and accept that, whether you want it or not, I *will* have an involvement in your pregnancy—and thereafter. All that is required, therefore, is for us to reach agreement on it. Starting with your accommodation. I will find an apartment for you, where you can live at least until the baby is born. We can use the time to discuss what is to happen once he or she makes an appearance.'

She didn't answer...only took a slug of her elderflower spritzer.

He went on talking. At least she wasn't arguing back, or giving him her pungent, if entirely irrelevant, opinion of him.

'I will cover all the expenses of the apartment—rent, taxes, utilities and so forth. I am also willing to make you an adequate monthly allowance to cover your costs during your pregnancy. I will also cover private medical costs for you, so you are not reliant on the NHS.'

She made no reply—only set down her glass, and picked up her knife and fork again.

An impulse just to get up and walk away knifed through him, but with rigid self-discipline he repressed it. This was not a situation he could walk away from.

Nor for the rest of my life.

He thrust the thought from him. He could not deal with it—not right now. It was enough just to handle the situation at hand.

He made himself continue. 'I was thinking that the

Holland Park area might be suitable. It is not far from Notting Hill, and your friend Megan, and it also has close access to the park there, which will be pleasant for you. How does that sound?'

He strove to make his voice civil.

Her response was an indifferent glance.

Something snapped inside him.

He dropped his cutlery abruptly.

'Do you think you might *possibly* bring yourself to pay attention? Bring yourself to deal with this situation—unprecedented for both of us—in a way that is co-operative and not intransigent?' he demanded scathingly, his patience at an end. 'I have acknowledged paternity, I am acknowledging my responsibilities for the child, and I am doing my damnedest to make your life easier so that you can have a healthy and safe pregnancy! So damn well stop stonewalling me!'

That got a response. She looked across at him. Anger was flaring in her eyes again.

'Am I supposed to be grateful? I *forced* myself to come to your office that day. Forced myself! I didn't want to—I didn't want anything more to do with a man who hadn't even had the courtesy to behave with some basic level of civility after our night together! But I thought that I should tell you—thought that I had no right to deny you knowledge of your own child. And all I got for my pains was insults and contempt! If you had said then that a paternity test might be prudent, but in a polite and civil manner, then I would have understood. But you just went straight for the jugular! You couldn't wait to throw me out! Like I was dirt on your shoe! And now—now that you can't evade paternity—you have the temerity to talk about my being *co-operative*? Don't make me laugh!'

Vincenzo's face was set. 'That was then…this is now—we have to deal with the situation.'

'I *am* dealing with it! I'm telling you I want nothing from you and nothing more to do with you. I am telling you I absolve you of all and any paternal anything! So just leave me—walk out the way you walked out on me the morning after the night before! Leave me to get on with my pregnancy and raise my child.'

'The child is mine as well. You cannot ignore that.' Vincenzo's voice was terse.

'Believe me, I'll do my level best—I promise you!'

She fell silent and drained the rest of her elderflower spritzer. Then she crushed her napkin onto her side plate and got to her feet.

'This has all been pretty pointless, but at least it's sorted things out between us. You go back to Italy and I'll look after myself. Like I say, I'll sign any documents you like, absolving you of any responsibility—especially financial—and then we'll be done with it all.'

She picked up her handbag, slung it over her shoulder, and prepared to walk away.

Vincenzo's next words stayed her. Where they came from, he did not know—but he heard himself say them all the same.

'There is an alternative outcome,' he heard himself say. 'That we marry.'

Siena stilled—and stared at him disbelievingly.

'We spend one night together—*one night*—and now you say we should *marry*?' Incredulity filled her voice.

'As I say, it would be one way of addressing the situation. Of course I would require you to sign a prenup, but since you have been at pains to tell me you are not interested in my money, that should not be a problem for you.'

She could hear the open sarcasm in his voice, and it grated like nails on a chalkboard.

Her eyes flashed. 'You must be insane to think I'd marry you!'

'Then accept my offer of accommodation and an allowance.'

His voice was implacable, his gaze on her relentless.

She sat down heavily again, placing her hands on the table either side of her empty plate, and leaned forward. There was a tangled knot of emotions inside her...like a bunch of snakes.

'I will say this one more time.' She spoke slowly, in a staccato voice, enunciating each word as if it was bitten out of her. 'I do not want anything more to do with you. I should never have had anything to do with you in the first place! I bitterly, *bitterly* regret that night!'

He was looking back at her, his face grim, eyes dark.

'Do you think I don't?' he retorted starkly. 'But it happened. And now we have to deal with the consequences. You will have to accept that you carry my child,' he said, and his darkened eyes had a dangerous anger in them. 'And you are not walking away with it.'

He drew a breath—a harsh, heavy one. That dark expression was still on his face, and she didn't like it. Not one little bit.

Suddenly, it was all too much. She couldn't cope— not one minute longer. Not with one more vicious, biting exchange.

She heaved herself to her feet. She was done here. Done, done, done, and *done* with Vincenzo Giansante.

She stood, her face working, and he looked back at her.

'Go to hell,' she said. 'Just go to *hell*!'

Then she walked out.

Before she collapsed.

CHAPTER FIVE

'So,' asked Megan, 'what are you going to do? Did he really offer to marry you?' Incredulity was mingled with another emotion—several of them, Siena thought cynically, of which envy was only one.

She gave an inner sigh. Megan was pitifully impressed by Vincenzo Giansante—that was obvious.

'It was a play, Megan, a totally transparent one. Marriage would give him control over me. And he must be insane to think I'd even give him the time of day!'

Megan laughed shortly. 'Any other woman would snap his hand off at the offer. All that money and all those lethal looks!'

'And all that charm…' Siena rejoined with acid sweetness.

'So, are you at least going to move into this apartment he's rented for you? He sent me the details—it looks pretty good.'

'No, of course I'm not,' Siena returned.

'But why not?' Megan pursued. 'Look, you can move in at the weekend—I'll help you.'

'Megan, no.' Siena's voice was adamant. 'That's final. I've got a roof over my head till Fran gets back—time enough to decide where I'm going to move to and get a place to rent there.'

Till then she'd stay here and keep on with her temporary clerical job at the PR firm Megan worked for, earning some useful money.

But when she got back from work on Friday evening, it was to find the bed in her room pulled away from the wall, all the furniture swathed in a dust sheet, another dust sheet on the floor, and paint pots on the chest of drawers.

Megan's attitude was unapologetic. 'I've decided this room needs a little sprucing up, Si.' Her tone was sympathetic, but determined. 'Just move into the apartment Vincenzo's taken for you—he's had the keys delivered to me, and I'll come with you this evening to settle you in. It's all furnished and kitted out. We just need to take basics, like milk and tea. We'll get a takeaway, and you can go food shopping tomorrow. I've even packed your things for you.'

Siena stared at Megan in dismay.

Megan patted her arm encouragingly. 'You know it makes sense, Si. It gives you somewhere to think things through. And I hope—I really, *really* hope—you'll decide to stay there and take up your place at art school. I'd hate to see you give it up!'

Siena's face worked. She knew her friend was trying to be helpful, but—

But right now, however galling it is, I have no choice but to do what she wants. I don't even have a bed to sleep in tonight!

Grimly, she let Megan have her way.

And Vincenzo Giansante was getting his own way too.

Her face darkened. She would stay in his damn flat *only* until she got her life sorted out. Then she'd be gone.

And he'll be out of my life.

The way, after all, he obviously wanted *her* out of *his* life...

Her expression became even grimmer, memory stabbing of how he'd walked out on her that morning after their searing night together.

He hadn't wanted anything more to do with her then, and if it weren't for the baby he still wouldn't. That was the blunt, hard truth of it...

Vincenzo gave a tight smile of grim satisfaction as he read Megan's text.

She's here—we're ordering a takeaway. She's not in the best mood, so I'd give her a day to accept what's happened.

He took her advice, waiting until Sunday before turning up at the apartment. As the taxi dropped him off he glanced around. The street on the park side of Holland Park Avenue was quiet and expensively residential. The apartment block was small and twentieth century, compared with the surrounding nineteenth-century stucco-fronted houses, but it was well maintained, and close to the park entrance. It was costing a pretty penny, but that was only a fraction of the future expense this whole damn situation would put him to.

A lifetime of expense. A lifetime of responsibility that he could not shirk, nor avoid. That he must assume, whatever it took. And right now that was getting Siena Westbrook to see sense.

That, at least, seemed to have started happening. She was here, in the apartment he'd taken for her. Now he had to move things on from there. Make some kind of acceptable arrangement for the future, however pointlessly and inexplicably obdurate she was being.

He frowned. Why had she not jumped at the financial offer he was prepared to make? Let alone his offer to marry her. His thoughts darkened. Why was she protesting? Refusing?

Well, whatever she was playing at, he would deal with it. He had no choice but to do so. This was not about her, or him. It was about the baby that in six months would be making its appearance. That was all he must focus on.

His expression as he paid off the taxi was set.

He had his own keys for the apartment, bestowed upon him by the letting agent, and he let himself into the lobby, ignoring the lift and vaulting lightly up the two flights of stairs. Then, without pause for thought, because thoughts were only unwelcome, he let himself into the apartment.

From the hallway he could see into the reception room, from which came the sound of the television. He walked in.

Siena was lounging on the sofa, a cup of tea on the side table, a paperback beside her, and sunshine streaming in from the window overlooking the garden at the rear.

As he walked in she sat bolt upright.

'What the hell—?' The words broke from her, shock and consternation in her face.

Two emotions knifed through Vincenzo. One was the same grim satisfaction he'd felt when he'd learnt she'd moved in here, fight it though she had. The other was completely different.

It knifed through him again.

The sunshine was turning her hair to a glossy mahogany, glinting off it gloriously, and even though she was lounging in nothing more than pale blue cotton trousers and a yellow top, and hadn't done a thing to her face, he still felt his senses kick in response. The same kick that had come that first, fateful evening when he'd seen her for the first time. Seen her—and wanted her.

He crushed the reaction down. It had been that damn reaction that had brought him to this predicament now.

'Buongiorno,' he said civilly, though he could hear the jibe in his own voice.

She grabbed the remote for the TV, flicking it to mute. It was some old black and white Hollywood movie, he could see.

'What are you doing here? And why have you just let yourself in?' she demanded.

'I came to see how you've settled in,' he said. He glanced around the room. 'Does it suit you, this place?' he asked.

She glowered at him. 'No, because I didn't choose to be here—you fixed it with Megan.'

He didn't bother to reply.

'Do you have any coffee?' he asked.

'I'm pregnant—no caffeine or stimulants,' she answered, her voice clipped.

He went into the kitchen, resolving to have a coffee machine delivered before his next visit. As it was, he opted for tea—only to discover that that, too, was decaffeinated. He made himself a cup, then went back into the living room, cup in hand. She was still curled up on the sofa, looking tense and baleful.

He lowered himself into an armchair, crossed one leg over the other, and made a start on his cup of tea.

'Your friend Megan told me you have not lived in London long,' he opened. He was going to stay civil, whatever the provocation. Anything else was not helpful. 'You never did mention, when we first met, what you do for a living.'

He saw two reactions in her. One was a distinct flare of colour in her cheeks as he referred to the evening when they had first so fatefully encountered each other. The other was a tightening of her expression—as if she didn't want to expound on the subject.

'I've been doing some casual office work for the PR company Megan works for,' she replied, but he could tell she said it with reluctance.

'Do you plan to continue?' he asked. He kept his voice studiedly neutral.

'I don't know,' she replied. 'I don't know what I'll be doing. Other than having a baby.'

Vincenzo let his eyes rest on her a moment. So, here it was, then—what he had been expecting. For all her vehement protestations that she didn't want anything to do with him, she did, in fact, expect him to keep her.

He didn't reply, only went on calmly sipping his tasteless tea. Letting his gaze rest on her. Letting himself be deflected from his purpose by something that was completely irrelevant.

She truly is beautiful—radiantly so.

His glance went to her waistline. Nothing showed. Yet within her body his child was growing...

He felt something go through him, but he did not know what it was. He set it aside. He had enough to deal with.

He finished his tea. On the still silent screen he could see the old film end, and Siena reached absently for the remote and turned the TV off.

He got to his feet. 'It's a fine afternoon—pleasantly warm for England. How about taking a walk in the park?' he asked.

He crossed over to the sofa, picked up her own empty tea mug, and took them both through into the kitchen. Then he returned to the living room. She hadn't moved.

She looked up at him. 'You've seen I'm OK, so why don't you leave now?'

'Because,' he said pointedly, his gaze levelled on her just as pointedly, 'we have things to discuss.'

Her face tightened. 'No,' she said, 'we do not.'

Vincenzo took an impatient breath. 'Stonewalling is pointless. There are practicalities to be decided upon.'

She shook her head vigorously. 'No, there are not. I am only in this damn flat until I find somewhere else. After that you can wash your hands of me.'

'But not,' he said even more pointedly, his gaze boring down at her, 'of the baby.'

Anger flashed in her eyes—and frustration too, he could see. She opened her mouth again, and he was pretty sure she was going to offload the same diatribe—tell him that she wanted nothing to do with him, that he should clear out and get back to Italy.

Well, that was not going to happen, and she had better take that on board.

He held up a hand.

'Let us walk and talk at the same time,' he said, making an effort to keep his voice even. He gestured towards the door. 'Shall we?' he said.

She got to her feet with visible ill grace, slipping her feet into the canvas shoes on the rug in front of the sofa. Silently he handed her her bag, lying on a sideboard within his reach. She all but snatched it. He went through into the entrance hall, holding open the door for her. She marched through, head high, making straight for the stairs. Vincenzo locked the door and followed her.

Of all the women in the world he knew, of every one of them with whom he had ever had sexual relations, it was this bristling, critical, obstreperous and supremely unco-operative and unappreciative one that he'd got pregnant.

He couldn't have made a worse choice.

But we did not choose, did we? We got landed with it, that's all. And now, somehow, I have to try and find a way forward.

That was all he must focus on.

As they made their way into Holland Park Siena was churning inside. Vincenzo walking in like that had been a shock, unexpected and totally unwelcome. Why the hell couldn't the man stay away? Stay in Italy. Wash his hands of the whole damn business, like she kept telling him to. He should be *glad* she didn't want anything to do with him!

Her eyes darkened. He thought her a slut for falling into bed with him the way she had, and now a gold-digger, trying to get a free meal ticket off him because she was pregnant.

*Well, I am neither, thank you! And you—*her glance

went malevolently to him as he fell into step beside her, heading towards the nearby park—*are a total jerk!*

She waited for anger to fill her again—the anger that had been spearing in her ever since that hideous afternoon when she'd been thrown out of his office. It had more than enough, to feed on. And yet right now all she could feel was a deflation of her spirits. A dullness and tiredness and sense of depression.

About everything—just *everything.*

This was all wrong. Wrong, wrong, *wrong.* She should not be pregnant, and she shouldn't be staying in an apartment which the man responsible had forced her into—the man who obviously thought she was after his money.

This wasn't what I wanted—none of it!

Even as she thought it she felt guilty, and that only added to her darkness of mood. The creation of new life was precious—she should not feel so bitter, should not so resent what had happened. How could her poor, innocent, hapless baby be to blame for anything? How could she blight the start of its existence by wishing she were not pregnant at all?

Yet still something cried within her.

This is not how it should be!

Babies should be born into joy and happiness, welcomed and rejoiced over, bringing blessings and being infinitely blessed themselves. To grow in love, become happy, healthy children…

Yet the cry inside her came again.

This is not how it should be!

But this time it was an echo. A terrifying echo. She felt it clutch within her, like a vice around her heart, her lungs, her throat. Memory stabbed at her, infinitely painful.

'What is it?'

Vincenzo's voice pierced her dark thoughts. He was walking beside her, along one of the paths in the park.

She didn't answer, and he spoke again. 'What is it,' he repeated.

She gave a shake of her head. 'It's nothing,' she said.

She didn't want to talk to him, to walk with him, to be with him at all. She wanted absolutely nothing in her life right now—the life that had finally been heading in the direction she had waited so long for it to go in, and which had now been derailed. *Again.*

She felt her arm taken, and halted in her pacing. Vincenzo stepped in front of her, looking down at her. His face had a taut expression.

'It is not "nothing",' he said. 'It is not "nothing" that both you and I find ourselves in a situation neither of us wished for.'

'No? But you think I'm definitely thinking it's a bit of luck for me, don't you? It's got my greedy little fingers into your nice rich pie, hasn't it? A meal ticket for life! That's what you think!'

His brow darkened and he dropped her arm.

Siena's mouth set tight. 'Despite my repeatedly telling you to walk away—that I don't need your financial support or want it!'

'So how will you support yourself?' he countered immediately. 'Live on state benefits in a council-paid bedsit? That was the graphic image painted by your friend Megan to get my attention,' he said witheringly.

'She acted totally without my consent!' Siena threw back instantly. 'I never wanted her to interfere. Just as I never wanted you to come anywhere near me again!

And just as I do *not* want any of your damn money!' she bit out. 'Just believe me when I say I've got enough to live on.' She took a slicing breath. 'If you really want to know, I've inherited some money and it's safely banked. It's quite enough to let me live somewhere a lot cheaper than London and look after my baby, so I neither need, let alone want, a single penny from you!'

Dear God, how many times had she got to say that before he got the damn message?

But it seemed he was set on moving on to a new subject.

'Even setting that aside—for the moment at least,' he said repressively, 'there is more to the situation than financial considerations.' Vincenzo's voice was still tight. 'I told you I would not walk away—and I do not mean only from my financial responsibilities.'

Siena started to walk again. The vistas of the park all around were scenic, but she had no appreciation for them.

Vincenzo fell into pace beside her again. 'We cannot avoid looking ahead,' he was saying now, as if he were forcing himself to do so. 'To beyond the child's birth and babyhood.'

She felt her mind sheer away. She couldn't even cope with being pregnant, let alone thinking beyond it to an unimaginable future. One she had never, in all her days, thought she would be landed with.

Depression weighed down on her. All around were people enjoying the park—families, couples, singletons young and old. Yes, maybe they had their own problems, but all she could focus on were her own. Her pace slowed, energy draining from her.

At her side, Vincenzo spoke again, glancing at her. 'We should find a café, and you should sit down,' he said.

They made their way to one with outdoor seating which overlooked a small fountain, and Siena was glad to sit down. Her energy levels fluctuated these days—her mental energy levels too. She knew it was not good for her to be so agitated—but what else could she be in the circumstances?

Vincenzo got coffee for them both, and she sipped her decaf without enthusiasm. As he sat opposite her at the small table she was acutely conscious of his physical closeness, the strength of his body, and she caught the scent of masculine aftershave. Memory assailed her, of that night she'd succumbed to his seduction.

I went along with it willingly—oh, so willingly! And now...

'Do you have to drink decaf all the time?' There was a frown on Vincenzo's face as he put the question to her.

'Standard recommendation when pregnant,' she said flatly, resenting the note of criticism. 'Like no alcohol and no smoking.'

'Is it so very bad for you?' Vincenzo pursued, stirring his own coffee. 'Pregnant women have drunk caffeinated tea and coffee for generations and no harm seems to have been done. The rules seem very strict these days. Banning all alcohol too...'

She gave a shrug, not wanting to debate it. She hadn't issued the damn guidelines, so why should he be challenging her? It set her teeth on edge.

'We are supposed to do nothing that risks the baby,' she said. 'Even though—'

She broke off.

Some risks have nothing to do with the mother's lifestyle...

No, she must not think of that—it was too upsetting. And it served no purpose but to weigh her down yet more. She knew she should—she must—be thankful, but the thought oppressed her all the same, however stringently she sought to repress the memories that assailed her. It made her feel guilty that she was resenting a pregnancy that was seemingly healthy when—

Vincenzo was speaking again, bringing her thoughts back to her predicament. Once again Siena got the impression he was choosing his words carefully,

'Stress is also bad. Stressful emotions.'

She eyeballed him, feeling on edge again. 'What are you getting at?'

He looked directly at her. 'Anger, hostility, resentment—these are all negative emotions. They cannot be doing you any good. Nor the baby.'

'Are you *criticising* me?' Siena's anger shot to the fore. 'Don't you damn well preach at me!'

He held up a hand. 'Do you deny that you are seething with anger at me?' he returned implacably. 'That that is your dominant reaction to me ever since your friend Megan took matters into her own hands to bring me here?'

Her eyes flashed with the very anger he was accusing her of. 'How should it be otherwise?' she threw at him witheringly. 'After that delightful scene in your office!'

A dismissive expression filled his face. 'What were you expecting?' he retorted scathingly, his expression hardening. 'You turn up, out of the blue, demand to see me, then drop your bombshell on my desk. Were you expecting me to shout with joy and sweep you into my arms and promise undying love?'

'I was expecting *civility*,' she ground out tightly—as tightly as she was gripping her coffee cup.

He made a rough sound in his throat, as dismissive as his expression. 'I dealt with the situation as required. Rationally. Until paternity was established, there was no point in any further conversation at that time.' He sat back, took a mouthful of his coffee. 'But now that it is established we can move forward—as we must.'

His gaze levelled on her.

'Tell me, have you thought through what I put to you the other evening? That one option appropriate to the situation would be that we marry.'

Siena stared at him. 'Even as a joke, that is not humorous. As a serious suggestion—and I cannot believe it to be as such—it is, as I've told you already, *totally* insane!'

She saw his face darken. He hadn't liked her answer, and it was obvious why. Presumably she should be melting all over him and planning a hideously expensive wedding as an excuse to start spending all his money on herself.

'There are practical advantages—' he began.

'No,' she said. She wanted this conversation stopped—right now.

His dark eyes flashed angrily and he held up a hand. 'Hear me out before you give me an infantile rejection! Marriage would regularise the situation…provide far more security both for yourself and the baby, and enable us to—'

'I said *no*,' Siena ground out. Her own eyes flashed with anger. 'The *only* reason you want to marry me is to control me—and my baby. So don't feed me any garbage to the contrary!'

For a moment she saw an expression on his face that almost silenced her. But she would not be silenced—she would *not*! Emotions were boiling up in her, tangled and knotted, vehement and vicious.

'It's bad enough you feel you have any say about my baby—let alone expect me to walk into the noose you're dangling in front of me. So get this, and get this once and for all—finally! I will *never* marry you! I will *never* have anything to do with you of my own free will. Because of this baby I am handcuffed to you—shackled to you! And I resent it and I hate it. *Hate* it—'

She broke off, churning inside. Heart thudding. She pushed her pallid, undrunk coffee aside. She got to her feet, looked down at him. Her face contorted with the emotion heaving inside her.

'I can't *bear*,' she said, 'that it's you who got me pregnant.'

She walked away. Eyes blind. Crushed and hopeless.

Words went through her head—as crushed and hopeless as her spirit.

It's all a mess—such a mess.

Such a hopeless, hopeless mess.

CHAPTER SIX

VINCENZO SAT AT his desk in his office in Milan. He should be working, but he wasn't. He was brooding. That was the only word for it. His expression was a study—a darkened one—and his hands were resting tightly on the arms of his custom-made leather chair. His eyes were seemingly fixed on a focal point that did not actually exist in the spacious, beautifully appointed and ferociously expensively decorated executive office, with its modernistic grey leather sofas facing each other across a low chrome and glass coffee table, backed by the floor-length plate glass window looking out over the city skyline.

In his head was circling the memory of visiting Siena two days ago. Baleful and benighted. What had it achieved? Nothing. It had only sunk them further into the impossibility of their situation. A situation neither of them wanted.

His mouth thinned.

Shackled to each other—that was what she'd said. And that was the blunt truth of it, all right. This baby, that neither of them wanted, was handcuffing them to each other. He could resent the fact that it was so all he liked—but it changed nothing.

Nothing could change the situation.

His hands tightened over the leather arms of his chair. He was trying, damn it. Trying to take the necessary responsibility, to make the necessary plans for the future. What else could he do? And for his pains she was stonewalling him totally. How did he get past that? How did he get her to drop her relentless hostility towards him? Because somehow he had to...

Resolve steeled in him. Anger, as he had said to her face, was her predominant emotion towards him—well, he had to defuse it. Bring down that wall of implacable hostility. Do whatever it took to do so.

He reached forward, lifted his desk phone, and spoke to his PA in the outer office. He told her to cancel the week's appointments and book him a flight to London tomorrow morning.

He was going back. Whether Siena Westbrook liked it or not, wanted him or not, he was going back.

Not for him, and not for her, but for the one person who was overweeningly more important than anything he or she might want—who deserved better than a pair of angry, hostile, irresponsible adults throwing their resentment at each other.

The baby she carried.

The only thing that mattered in all this sorry mess.

Siena was kneeling on the floor, leafing through her portfolio, her spirits sinking as she did so. So short a time ago her future had been bright, finally taking off. And now it had crashed and burned. She had given up on her future once before—and now she was doing it again. Instead of looking forward to starting a new term she was scouring the Internet for affordable rental properties in places—anywhere at all—where she might want to live as a single mother of the baby that was on the way.

With a sigh she leant the portfolio back against the wall of her bedroom, then leaned back herself as well, stretching out her legs. Her hands went to her midriff. Already there was a change in her body—a rounding discernible to her, even if her clothes still hardly showed it. Within her body a hapless little baby was forming, day by day, its tiny body taking shape, limbs and organs and tissues and heartbeat…so desperately tiny, so desperately vulnerable…

So entirely and totally dependent on me.

A wave of fierce protectiveness went through her, and her fingers splayed out like a net to keep safe the tiny soul inside her.

Poor little mite… None of this is your fault, yet you are going to be the one who suffers—born to two irresponsible, selfish people who thought their own fleeting sexual pleasure so important…

She looked out across the room, but she did not see it at all. Her face was a mask of self-condemnation. Yes, she wished with all her being that she had never conceived that wretched night, but it had happened, and now she must do whatever it took not to blight the totally innocent life within her.

I've got to protect you…make it better for you, little one. I've got to! Make the best I can out of the mess that this is. I've got to at least try. I owe you that…

And if that meant coping—somehow—without getting so angry, so upset, so destructively emotional with Vincenzo...well, she would have to.

Because only one person mattered now. And it wasn't her, and it certainly wasn't Vincenzo Giansante.

Her hands pressed protectively again.

It's you, little one—only you...

Vincenzo's fingers hovered over the text message he was composing. Siena had walked out on him twice now—in the restaurant and in the park. He had to get past that. Get past the wall of her hostility.

Would what he intended achieve that? Well, he would find out soon enough.

He reread the message, then hit 'send'.

I am back in London. I would like to come and see you again. I have something to say that needs to be said.

The reply came briefly.

What is it?

He tapped back.

In person. This evening? I will come to the apartment for eight.

Her reply took longer. But it came, and at least that was something.

You're paying the rent. I can't stop you.

His mouth tightened. Would she even be there?

* * *

Siena was pacing up and down. It was seven fifty-seven, and she was on edge. She didn't want to see Vincenzo again. And at the same time she knew she must.

I can't just pretend he doesn't exist. I might want to, but I can't. And whatever it is that he says he wants to say to me, I need to know it.

He was, as she knew, a man perfectly prepared to be ruthless. Ruthless enough to not even stick around for breakfast with her that morning after the night before. Ruthless enough to say to her what he had when she'd told him she was pregnant. Ruthless enough to throw her out of his office. Ruthless enough to threaten her with the law when she refused to co-operate on a paternity test. Ruthless enough to rent this flat and then commandeering Megan into manipulating her into moving in to it.

Ruthless all round.

A sudden longing to pour herself a glass of wine and knock it back assailed her. Going without alcohol was hard when it came to moments like this. She wondered whether to make herself a cup of tea, and see if that helped at all, but she didn't have time to drink it. He would be punctual, she knew.

He was. She heard the front door open and turned around, facing the door into the hall.

Vincenzo walked in.

She felt tension bite inside her—or something bite, at any rate. Every time she saw him she felt his impact.

No wonder I fell for him—fell into bed with him...

No, there was no point thinking that, or remembering it. It was, after all, what caused her to be standing here now, nerves on edge, in an apartment whose rent she couldn't have afforded for a week, let alone a month, and pregnant by the man now walking into the room.

He was wearing a business suit, pale grey, perfectly tailored with Italian flair to his lean, tall frame. His shirt was white, his tie pale grey, his hair clipped short. His features possessed whatever chemistry it was that made her—and doubtless every other female—gulp openly.

Not that she did—but she could feel the impulse to do so all the same.

She crushed it down. Vincenzo had turned up to talk to her—he had something to say, he'd said. She had to brace herself for it.

And I won't let myself be upset by it—whatever it is. I won't—I can't! I have to think not about myself, only about my baby.

That was the resolve she'd made, sitting by the now useless portfolio that had won her a place at art school she could no longer take up. Letting Vincenzo upset her wasn't good for her—let alone the baby. Vincenzo himself had told her that—and, gall her though it did, he was right.

I have to stay calm—not let my emotions boil over. Whatever he throws at me.

His eyes—dark, long-lashed and quite unreadable, so no change there, she thought resignedly—were resting on her.

'How are you?' he asked, his voice cool and accented.

'The baby,' replied Siena pointedly, because the question was not about her, and she knew that perfectly well, 'is fine.'

A frown flashed briefly, as though her answer, and the pointedness with which she'd made it, displeased him.

'And yourself?' he pursued.

She gave half a shrug. 'Fine,' she said. 'I'm having, it seems, a very healthy pregnancy.'

She took a breath, wanting to cut to the chase, not wanting to let her fragile, flammable emotions flare up when she was trying so hard to stay cool and calm—the way he was being. For now, at least.

'Your text said you had something to say to me.'

Tension had entered her voice. She could hear it. So, it seemed, could he. Because he made a slight gesture with his head, as if to negate her reaction.

'Yes, but not right now.' His voice was clipped. His stance changed, and so did his tone. 'Tell me, have you eaten?'

Siena shook her head. Was she supposed to provide dinner for him?

'In which case,' he went on, 'there's a restaurant nearby on Holland Park Avenue that appears tolerable.'

'OK…' she said guardedly.

Eating out was preferable to eating in—and, whatever it was that Vincenzo wanted to say, doing so in public might be preferable too.

She glanced at him. 'I had better change first,' she said.

She was wearing cotton pedal pushers and a long-sleeved tee shirt—not good enough for a swanky restaurant. Memory darted, of how she'd deliberately not dressed up the previous time. But that had been to make a point. A point she didn't need to make a second time.

'I'll be two minutes,' she said.

She kept to it, too, having simply swapped what she'd been wearing to a pair of smarter, dark blue trousers and a blue striped shirt, worn loose. She didn't think her pregnancy showed much, but it definitely wouldn't in the shirt. She didn't bother with make-up, simply brushed her hair, drawing it back with a barrette. Then, staring at her reflection, she grabbed some lip gloss after all and touched it to her lips. Then she stared again.

Memory intruded suddenly—of how Megan had dolled her up that fateful evening, for that swanky party at the Falcone. Squeezing her into that tight dress, doing her make-up—*over*doing it, by Siena's standards—leaving her hair loose and tumbling down her back, seeing her legs lengthened by the high heels she'd persuaded her to wear.

She'd looked totally vamped. Sex on legs...

It wasn't me.

It hadn't been her. The reflection that had gazed back at her that evening, with its deep eyes, lavishly lashed, scarlet mouth, wanton hair and skin-tight dress. Dressed to kill.

No wonder he thought I was up for it...

She swallowed. She *had* been up for it, hadn't she? She could hardly deny it.

She shut her eyes to block out the memory of what she'd looked like that evening. Then opened them again.

Now she looked nothing like that.

Thankfully...

She grabbed a cardigan, threw it around her shoulders, slipped her feet into flat pumps, and went back out. She didn't know what Vincenzo wanted to say to her, but she knew she had to be ready for it. She nerved herself accordingly.

He was by the sitting room window, looking out, his

face in profile to her. He looked severe, but as she came in he turned. Whatever he was thinking, she didn't have a clue.

He nodded, in lieu of saying anything, and crossed to the door, holding it open for her. She walked through into the entrance hall, opening the front door, picking up the handbag lying on a pier table next to it. They didn't speak as they went down to the lobby, nor as they went out onto the pavement. The sun had gone and it was very slightly chilly. She was glad of the cardigan.

He still didn't speak, and neither did she, as they paced beside each other heading for Holland Park Avenue.

The restaurant, looking swish enough for Vincenzo, was on their side of the busy road, and this early in the week was not full at this hour. She took her place at the table they were shown to, and then the business of presenting menus and ordering drinks took place, so it was some minutes before they were left alone.

Vincenzo glanced at the closed menu, but did not open it. Instead, he looked across at her. His face still had that reserved expression on it, now even more pronounced, and Siena felt a sudden shaft of apprehension. Whatever it was he'd come back to London to tell her, it was not going to be good. Nothing he ever said to her was good…

As she braced herself, Vincenzo's inexpressive gaze rested on her, quite unreadable. Then he spoke.

'I owe you an apology,' he said.

Vincenzo saw Siena's eyes widen. Whatever she'd been expecting, it hadn't been that. But then, he thought sardonically, that was hardly surprising. Had he not resolved to say it, he wouldn't have expected it himself.

'I owe you an apology,' he said again. He kept his gaze levelled on her. 'It has been owing to you,' he said, 'for some time.'

He paused, as if he might be waiting for her to say *What for?* But that look of surprise was still paramount in her widened eyes.

'I have behaved badly to you, for which I apologise.'

He took the slightest of breaths and kept going. This had to be done.

'My reception of the news you came to tell me in my office was not acceptable. I apologise for it completely. Unreservedly.'

There was silence. Complete silence.

Then Siena said slowly, 'You came to England to tell me this?'

'Yes,' he said.

The slightest frown creased her brow. 'Why?'

'Because,' he said, 'my apology has, as I say, been owing for some time.'

The frown did not lighten. 'Why now?' she said.

His right index finger smoothed along the length of the knife at his place-setting. He was trying to find the words—first in Italian, then in English—that would answer her question. They did not come easily. But they came all the same. Feeling his way with every one of them.

'Because...' He spoke carefully, feeling his way with every word, conscious of the tension in his voice, his jaw, his throat—his expression. His eyes were levelled, by an act of explicit will, on her closed and shuttered face. 'Because it was holding things back—holding us apart. Because...'

He made himself go on in the same tight and guarded

tone, saying what had to be said, what needed to be said, what was necessary for the future that only the words he was saying now could create. A future that had to exist. Because it was the only one that would do any justice to the reason she and he were yoked together as they were.

'Because without it, it will be impossible for us to have any kind of…acceptable relationship within the situation in which we both find ourselves.'

A glint was suddenly in her eye. A steely one.

'Do you mean it?' she asked. 'That apology?'

He would have had to have been deaf and stupid not to hear the edge in her voice—and he was neither. And he would have had to have been stupid indeed not to know that only one answer was permissible.

Whether or not I believe it myself does not matter. All that matters is the fact that it is the only means to the end I have to achieve.

'Yes,' he said. He paused, his eyes still levelled on her. 'Do you accept my apology?'

For a moment her face was unreadable, her eyes masked now. Then she spoke.

'Yes,' she said.

Siena heard herself say it, but she wasn't sure it was real—had she really said it?

But she had, and she knew why.

For the same reason he had brought himself to apologise to her. To make an apology she had never, for a moment, thought to hear.

But he'd made it all the same.

And I have to bring myself to accept that apology.

Because if she didn't…

Everything that had passed between them since the moment she'd walked into his London office to tell him she was pregnant flashed before her eyes. Every ugly, vicious, biting, hostile expression of enmity and anger. Of bitterness and resentment and loathing.

It was draining from her every residue of the energy she still possessed. Draining her and destroying her...

I can't go on like that—I just can't.

However justified her reaction to him...

I have to let it go—I have to.

It was the same sense of deeply unwilling resolve that had gone through her as she had sat by her portfolio, hunkered down on the carpet, her hands cradling the tiny, innocent life within her. It, alone of all involved in the situation, deserved to be their priority.

We've got to do this—Vincenzo and I. We don't want to—we wish each other to perdition. But we can't go there, either of us. Because it isn't just ourselves we'd be there...

She heard him speaking now, this man who was the other half of the tiny life growing inside her, depending on her so absolutely.

'Thank you,' he said.

The waiter was returning with their drinks. Vincenzo hadn't bothered with a cocktail—he would drink wine with the meal—and for now matched Siena with her obligatory soft drink. Iced water was placed on the table as well, along with rolls and butter.

'Shall we order?' Vincenzo said, opening his menu.

Siena did likewise.

It was a strange moment...a strange atmosphere. So

little had been said verbally—but he knew it was more than that. He felt as if he'd gone through a barrier that had not been visible, only tangible. Tension was still making his shoulders stiff, his expression severe, but now it came not from knowing that he had to say what he'd just said, but from not knowing how she would be with him now.

He busied himself scanning the menu options, giving her time to do likewise. Then, seeing her place hers flat on the table, closed his.

'Chosen?' he asked.

Memory suddenly hit him. That was exactly what he'd asked her when they'd removed themselves from that party to have dinner at the Falcone restaurant. When both of them had been radiating a force field neither could resist—nor had any wish to resist—and that searing sexual desire had flared between them.

For a second it almost overwhelmed him, the vividness of that memory, and of what it had led to when they'd been alone in his room, desire flaring...blazing to white-hot flame...

He slammed it down. Slammed down the memory as if to crush it out of existence.

Except its echo mocked him. The very fact that memory existed was the very reason he was here now...

With a start, he realised she was speaking.

'Yes, I'll have the sole Veronique,' she was saying.

He nodded, deciding almost at random on the lamb. Then he turned his attention to the wine list. A glass or two would suffice...no need to order a bottle.

'What will you drink?' he heard himself asking.

'Just another of these.' She indicated the glass she'd been sipping from.

'When will you be allowed alcohol again?' he asked.

This total ban seemed alien and unnecessary to him. Did pregnant women in Italy deprive themselves so? He had no idea—he did not socialise with pregnant women either in Italy or here, or anywhere. They were an unknown species to him.

'When I stop breastfeeding,' came the answer.

He looked across at her. 'You intend to breastfeed?' he asked.

He strove to keep the question neutral, not wanting her to pick up any criticism, implied or not, in any answer she might give. This entire purpose of the evening was his attempt—finally, wearily, resignedly—to get them beyond the warfare that raged between them.

Warfare that was as wearying as it was pointless.

In his head, memory stabbed again—not of the fateful night that had led to this moment, but of her words, hurled at him repeatedly, telling him that he should leave her and go back to Italy, get on with his life, have nothing more to do with her...

Or the child she carried.

His child.

Does she really want me to do that?

She was speaking again, and he made himself pay attention to her and not to his turbid thoughts.

'Yes, unless there's some kind of problem. It's nature's way, after all...breastfeeding. It helps the baby's immune system develop. And anyway—' she made a face '—from what I've read so far it seems to be a lot easier than faffing about with sterilising bottles all the time.'

'Does it not tie you to the baby?' Vincenzo heard himself ask.

She levelled a look at him. 'Since I don't have anything else planned *except* looking after my baby, that isn't exactly a problem,' she said.

He frowned. 'You mentioned previously that you'd inherited some money, so could afford to support a child.'

Whatever the sum was, judging from her clothes, it clearly did not run to anything lavish.

'Yes,' she acknowledged.

She added nothing more. He tried to draw her out.

'You never did tell me what your line of work is—other than temping at your friend's office.'

'No, I didn't,' she answered shortly.

He looked across at her, trying to recall their conversation that first night over dinner at the Falcone. But there had been nothing about her life in England. They'd talked about Italy in general, and the city she was named after but had never visited. She'd been interested, and made conversation, and had not been unintelligent in her questions to him.

The waiter was there, hovering, ready to take their orders, and it was a timely distraction. As the man departed, Vincenzo drew breath. He needed to keep going with this new, tenuous neutrality between them.

'So, what did you do before—?' he started, and then realised the only way to finish the sentence was by saying *before you found yourself pregnant by me.*

But he didn't have to say it. She said it for him.

'Before I found myself in this unholy mess?' she said.

She hadn't said it angrily, or accusingly. But there was a bleakness in her voice that he could not help but hear. He could feel it reaching him, settling around them like a thickening mesh, winding around them, binding them.

Another spike of memory came, from that episode in the park—her saying, so vehemently and so bitterly, that they were handcuffed together...shackled...

Rejection flared in him. He wasn't going back to that. He'd come here tonight specifically to get beyond that. Whatever it took.

'Does it have to be a mess?'

He heard the words fall from him.

CHAPTER SEVEN

SIENA'S EYES FLASHED to him.

'You have another name for it?'

She didn't say it angrily—she wasn't going to get upset. But she wasn't going to whitewash it either. 'Mess' was—bluntly and bleakly—the only word for the situation.

His eyes were levelled on her. She could not read them.

'I think,' he said, and his voice matched his eyes, his expression, 'that we must find one.' He paused, his eyes still on her. 'Because it is not…helpful to call it that. To think of it as that.'

She saw him take a breath, a thin one, and it pressed his mouth for a moment before he went on.

'We must get beyond it.'

His eyes dropped from her and he reached for his wine. For the second time that evening Siena wished she had a glass of wine to turn to as well. Instead, she took a mouthful of her soft drink, slightly effervescent. Memory shot through her of how the mousse of the champagne she'd knocked back at that fateful party had filled her mouth…her senses…her blood… Loosening her inhibitions, making her impulsive, adventurous, daring…

Reckless.

Landing her where she was now.

She set down her glass with a click, eyeballed Vincenzo.

'How?' she said bluntly.

There was a careful, watchful air about him as he answered her.

'We have made a start,' he said. 'I have given you an apology that you have accepted, and we are dining together in a civil fashion.' His mouth twisted suddenly. 'That is a definite start. Something to build on.'

She kept on eyeballing him. 'And just how,' she rejoined tautly, 'do you intend we do that?'

She could feel the tension building inside her again. She didn't want it to.

And now he was answering her, and she knew he was picking his words carefully.

'We should get to know each other better,' he said.

Siena's eyes widened. 'Really? Don't we know enough? The essentials? You are rich and I am pregnant. Isn't that what it boils down to? For you, at any rate.'

It was her turn to twist her mouth.

His expression changed again. As if what she'd said so bluntly had been more blunt than he would have preferred.

'I have already apologised to you on that score,' he said stiffly. 'So perhaps we could move on from there?' His tone was pointed.

'Move on to where?'

'As I say, to knowing each other better,' he replied.

She sat back. 'So, what do you want to know?'

If it helped to stop her tension rising, then she would go along with him. Maybe…

He lifted a hand slightly. 'Well, I made a start, asking you about your work. You chose not to answer me.'

She gave a shrug, helping herself to a bread roll. She was hungry suddenly. 'Because there isn't much to say. I don't have a glittering career—unlike Megan.'

'So what have you been doing with your life so far?' he continued.

She busied herself buttering her roll. She didn't want to talk about having hoped to go to art school. Let alone second time around. Let alone why it was second time around.

She felt memories from those anguished years seek to intrude, painful and difficult. But she must not let them. There was no reason now, in her condition—healthily pregnant—for such haunting, such apprehension.

It's nothing like it was for them—it's all quite different. Quite different for my baby…

Vincenzo was speaking again, and she found herself glad of the distraction from thoughts—fears?—she did not want to have.

'Did you grow up in London?' Vincenzo put to her.

Siena shook her head. This was safe enough, surely? 'No, I'm a country girl, born and bred.'

'What part of the country?' he pursued.

'East Anglia…a small country town.' Without her being conscious of it her voice softened as she remembered her happy childhood. 'My father was a vet, my mother his veterinary nurse. My brother trained as a vet too, ready to take over the practice in due course—' She broke off.

It wasn't that safe after all…

She was aware that Vincenzo was resting his gaze on her, and that it still had that careful, watchful quality to it.

'Have you told your family you are pregnant?' he asked.

'No,' she said. She tried not to let her voice sound short. 'My parents—'

She stopped, took another drink from her glass, her mouth suddenly dry. She looked away, out over the restaurant, which was now starting to fill up.

'My parents did *pro bono* work every year. My father was an equine vet, and he and my mother went out to North Africa regularly, to help at a donkey charity they supported. Donkeys are crucial to the livelihoods of most of the rural population in that part of the world—but sadly their owners often don't have the means to look after them properly. My parents gave their own services to the charity, and helped to train local practitioners as well. They did it for years… Except that one year—' She stopped again. Took a painful breath. 'One year, while they were out there, there was an earthquake.'

She felt her throat tighten, reached for her glass again.

'I'm sorry.'

She heard the words, spoken quietly, but she could not look at him. Nor could she say anything.

Into the silence he spoke again, careful still. 'You mentioned a brother—?'

'He lives in Australia,' she said quickly. 'We're not estranged or anything…' She could hear the awkwardness in her voice and tried to speak over it. 'But, well… it's the other side of the world.'

That was all she wanted to say. But inside her head

thoughts were running that she did not wish to think. Thoughts about her brother. At some point she must tell him that she was pregnant. It would not be easy...

She looked up at Vincenzo, setting down her knife. 'What about you?' she asked, turning the tables on him. Deflecting questions away from herself.

Did she even want to know anything about him?

If they were going to get beyond their destructive, exhausting hostility she must make an effort to.

He's apologised—I've accepted it. Now we move on.

He did not get a chance to answer her. At that moment their food was arriving, and Siena quickly made a start on her fish. It was delicate, and delicious, the tiny new potatoes and fresh peas served separately equally delicious. Across from her Vincenzo was eating his lamb—which looked, to her mind, too rare for her palette.

'How is your sole?' Vincenzo asked politely.

'Very good,' she answered, equally politely.

For a few minutes they did nothing but make inroads into their dinner, then Vincenzo resumed their conversation.

'You asked about me,' he said, picking up on the question she'd turned on him. He took another forkful of lamb before he went on.

Was it an effort for him as well? Siena wondered. His voice sounded stilted, but he was answering her all the same.

'I cannot claim to be a country boy—I grew up in the suburbs of Milan. My background was not as...' She heard him hesitate suddenly, then continue. 'Not as affluent as my life is now. I have improved it since then.'

Siena looked across at him. There had been an edge

to his voice as he'd finished that sentence—she'd have had to be deaf not to hear it.

'How?' she asked.

His wealth was clearly of prime importance to him, and he guarded it from wannabe pregnant gold-diggers, so presumably it was a subject dear to his heart—and his ego.

And his fears…

Just in case I get my sticky, greedy little fingers into it…

'Hard work,' he came back succinctly. 'I studied, took an interest in economics and finance—because that, after all, is where the money is. I worked to earn money during the day and studied by night. I got my qualifications, and went to work for one of Milan's finance houses—it is the financial centre of Italy, as well as its fashion capital—and then, when I felt I had learnt enough to try and make my own fortune, I set up for myself.'

She looked at him, frowning slightly. 'What is it exactly that you do?'

'I make investments,' he said. 'I started by using my own money to accumulate sufficient funds by making investments on the Milan stock exchange. Then I used profits from that to invest in other companies, other ventures. I persuaded others to contribute as well, and made money for them as well as myself. Money,' he said, and now Siena could hear not just an edge, but a dryness to his voice, 'makes money. Once you have it, it is easy to make more of it.'

His voice changed, and now the dryness had gone, but not the edge. The dryness was replaced by something that might even have been bitterness.

'The challenge is the initial capital formation,' he said. 'That is where the hardest work is.'

'You started from nothing?' she asked.

She saw him reach for his wine, take a mouthful, set the glass back with a decided click.

'More or less,' he said.

There was no mistaking the bitterness in his voice now. She let her eyes rest on him. His face had closed—that was the only word for it. Instinctively, she moved the subject away.

'You asked about my family,' she said. 'What about yours?'

But his expression remained closed and he turned his attention to his lamb.

'None worth mentioning,' he answered tersely.

Then he set his knife and fork down abruptly, looked straight across at her. There was a strange expression in his eyes now, one she could not make out.

'Apparently,' he said, 'we have something in common. Neither of us comes with a large family around us.'

Words rose in Siena's head. Words she did not want to hear and would not say. But they said themselves inside her head for all that.

Yet between us we are making a family.

Immediately, instantly, she refuted them—rejected them. No, that was *not* what they were doing. There was nothing of 'family' about their situation. Nothing at all.

We are strangers who fell into bed in a moment of reckless, unthinking lust—and that does not, cannot, must not, should not have anything at all to do with 'family'!

She broke eye contact, dipped her head again. She got

stuck back into her sole Veronique…stabbed a potato with the tines of her fork.

As if she could stab the words that had just forced their impossible, unnecessary and totally *wrong* way into her head.

Vincenzo heard his own words echo in his head.

'Apparently we have something in common.'

His mouth tightened.

Something else besides the child she carries.

Doggedly, he went on eating, though for an instant the tender lamb tasted like cardboard in his mouth. He swallowed it down, reached for his wine. This whole evening had been his idea, and he must stick with it. It was…necessary.

Necessary to have made that apology to her, whether or not he'd meant it.

Necessary to attempt civil conversation with her.

Necessary for them to talk to each other. Get to know each other.

Because one day soon we will be parents.

It seemed impossible to believe that a single night had turned them into what they would be for the rest of their lives.

He pulled his mind away, finished off his lamb, pushed his plate away from him. He took another mouthful of wine. Time to make conversation again. To get to know each other a bit more. The way they had to.

He frowned inwardly. Her parents had been professionals, and so was her brother, it seemed. Had she really not done anything similar? Just worked as a clerk, or whatever, in her friend's office?

He gave a shrug mentally. What did it matter? She wasn't going to be working at all now. Courtesy of her pregnancy and his wealth.

No, don't go there again. It is as it is. You will be funding her existence because you are funding the existence of the child that is yours. And you can afford it, so if she benefits from it, why care?

She had finished her fish and the waiter was gliding up again, carefully placing the dessert menus on the table, whisking away the empty dishes.

Vincenzo picked up his menu. 'Do you care for dessert?' he asked.

Memory shot through him again. That night at the Falcone she had ordered an iced *parfait*, he recalled now. And he had watched her spooning little mouthfuls, openly relishing them. He recalled that frisson now, untimely and unwelcome though it was, of watching her sensuous enjoyment. It had only fuelled his impatient desire for her, his wanting the meal to be over and the real purpose of being with her that night to begin.

He put the memory from him. It was inappropriate.

She'd picked up her menu, was scanning it assiduously.

'I'm torn,' she said. 'There's a lot to choose from...' she mused.

'I see there is a raspberry parfait on offer. You had something similar at the Falcone,' Vincenzo heard himself saying, and instantly wished he had not.

Yet even as he cursed himself for referencing that fateful evening he became aware of something else he wished he had not done. And it wasn't about the unwelcome outcome of that night.

It was about what had led to it in the first place.

Now that wall of hostility that had been there since she'd walked into his office to drop her bombshell all those weeks ago had gone, other things were taking its place. Things he did not want. Oh, he wanted a degree of basic civility between them—just as he'd told her when he'd made himself apologise, and when he'd said they must get beyond it—but now more was happening. Some line of self-defence had been breached. Something he'd been holding at bay. Something their mutual hostility had kept at bay...

But now it was running again...

He felt his gaze fasten on her. Though she looked very different from the way she'd looked at that party, her image now—nothing like a siren flaunting her sexuality—did not mean he could not see just how appealing her looks were. She might be wearing no make-up to enhance those blue-green eyes of hers, she might have her hair drawn back into a simple ponytail, and she might be wearing an open-necked shirt not designed for allure, but he was increasingly aware that it did nothing to detract from what nature had endowed her with.

If anything, it enhances it—shows off her natural beauty...

He felt it reach to him—not with the full-on, seductively sensual allure he'd been unable and unwilling to resist indulging in that night at the Falcone, but with a pull that made him want to go on letting his eyes fasten on her, appreciate what she had on show.

It was having an effect on him—an effect he did not want. Because it was irrelevant. His attraction to her, overpowering as it had been that night, was what had landed him in this situation—the very last thing he wanted now was for that to rear its head again.

He shifted in his seat, forcing his gaze away, wishing to God he'd not made that damn remark about their dinner together that evening.

'In which case I'll definitely avoid it!' he heard her say, and by the way she said it she knew she had found the reference unwelcome as well.

His mouth tightened again. Something else they apparently had in common...

Not wanting to remember that night—think about it at all...

The waiter had glided up again, ready to take their orders. Vincenzo specified cheese, in a voice curter than he would usually have used. Then he heard Siena say, her voice as tight as before, 'And for me the *tarte citron*.'

She handed her menu back.

'And coffee,' she added. 'Decaf. Thank you.' Her voice was staccato now.

Vincenzo, not looking at her, ordered coffee for himself. 'Not decaf,' he stipulated.

The waiter moved off again.

For a moment there was silence.

Vincenzo cast about for something neutral, anodyne to say. The trouble was he couldn't think of anything.

As if she had come to the same conclusion, Siena spoke abruptly. 'So, we don't really have anything to say to each other, do we?' she said.

She reached for her glass, drank from it and set it down again. Looked across at him.

Her blue-green eyes, so striking, so expressive, were now expressing something caustic.

'So there's no point us trying to get to know each other, is there?' she went on, her voice caustic too.

Vincenzo dragged his thoughts from her eyes and frowned slightly. 'I'm not used to getting to know people,' he heard himself say tightly.

He saw Siena's expression change. Become veiled.

'Especially women?' she said. 'After all, what's the point in getting to know them? You won't be sticking around, so why bother?'

The hostility was back in her voice, in her face.

His own face tightened. This was *not* what he wanted. His resolve not to make any reference back to their searing night together vanished. This was another part of her wall—like it or not—and he had to dismantle it if he could. In the same way as before.

'Do you want an apology for that, too?' he asked. 'For not staying to have breakfast with you?' He didn't wait for a response, but spoke bluntly. 'It wasn't possible. I had a business meeting at eight-thirty, and after that meetings back to back all day—it's what I do when I come to London: max out my time here. And as for that eight-thirty meeting—I had made the appointment,' there was a caustic note in his voice too now, 'long before I met you.' There was an infinitesimal pause. 'I had not envisaged that the previous night would be as it was.'

She broke eye contact. 'Make that both of us,' she said. Then, almost immediately, her eyes flashed back to his. Full-on. 'Despite your charming assumption that it's a way of life for me.'

Antagonism bit in every word.

Vincenzo stilled.

'I believe,' he said tightly, 'that my original apology to you covered that issue.'

'Did it?' Her challenge was open.

'Yes.' He spoke with precision. 'However, if you wish me to clarify, I herewith apologise for any inference I drew that you make a habit of spending the night with men you have only just met, so that identifying the one who might be responsible for any consequent pregnancy would require extensive paternity testing. It was a slur on your character as unmitigated as it was unwarranted.'

He paused again, then half lifted an eyebrow.

'Will that do?' he said.

She didn't say anything but he could see her face working, as if conflicting emotions were cutting across it. He saw her swallow painfully. On an impulse he didn't understand, he let his hand start to reach towards her, then he pulled it back.

He spoke again. But in a different tone of voice now.

'Look, shall we just accept and believe that each of us acted out of character that night? That, for whatever reason, our id got the better of us—if you want to analyse it in Freudian terms. That seems as good a way as any, but do choose any other that makes sense to you personally. We succumbed to something we very probably would never have done under other circumstances. And…' he drew a breath '…if we accept that, then maybe we can also accept that what happened just happened, for whatever reason, and put it behind us.'

Even as he spoke, making himself sound reasonable and rational, he was conscious of a level of hypocrisy deep within him. But he set it aside. The fact that whether she was dressed to kill, as she had been that night, or dressed deliberately plainly, as she was on the present occasion, her looks would always draw his attention was completely irrelevant to the current situation…

I have to ignore that. Because it is the very last thing that I can allow into the situation we are trying to deal with.

He could see the same conflicting reactions playing across her face.

'I did put it behind me,' she said.

Her voice was low. Troubled. She wasn't making eye contact with him, but looking down at the tablecloth.

'It was the only way I could deal with it. Deal with what had happened. What I had *let* happen.' Abruptly, her eyes flashed back up to him. 'I made myself angry,' she said. 'I made myself angry about the way you walked out the next morning. Angry with you so that…' She paused, her face working again. 'So that I didn't have to be angry with myself for what I'd done.' She drew a breath. 'Because what happened that night was something that has *never* happened to me before. And…and it shocked me. Shocked me that I'd done it.'

Her face contorted suddenly and she squeezed her eyes shut, as if she were shutting out the world. Shutting him out with it.

Vincenzo's hand moved again, and this time he did not draw it back. Instead, he very lightly—very briefly—touched her cheek. Then he took his hand away.

'There is no need to beat yourself up about it,' he said.

His voice sounded different—he could hear it—but didn't know why. Didn't know why he had made that impulsive gesture of…

Of what?

Comfort? Was that it? Or collusion. Maybe that was it.

'And if it's any consolation,' he went on, 'you've probably pretty much described my own reaction.'

His voice was dry, but it was not dry with the acerbic tone he'd used before. This was self-knowledge. Belated self-knowledge. He, too, had used his anger at her—anger whipped up when she'd come to his office to tell him she was pregnant—to disguise his own shock that he had fallen into bed with a woman within hours of meeting her.

She had unscrewed her eyes, unscrewed her face, and was looking across at him now. Something had changed in her face.

'Men always think that it's OK to slut-shame a woman,' she said. 'While they themselves stay squeaky-clean and fragrant...'

Her voice had an edge—and with cause, he acknowledged.

He gave half a smile...a twisted one. 'Then they are hypocrites,' he said. 'And that applies just as much now, in the twenty-first century, as in any earlier period when women's sexuality was used as a weapon against them.'

He took a breath—a heavy one, but a releasing one too. Looked across at her. There was an open expression on her face now, and her eyes were meeting his. For the first time there was neither hostility in them nor challenge, nor reserve or guardedness.

'Siena,' he said, and he used her given name for the first time that evening, 'let's just accept what happened, shall we? We acted out of character that night, both of us. For whatever reason, it happened. Let's make peace with it.' He moved on, because it seemed the natural thing to do now. 'Just as we should make peace with your being pregnant and all that entails. We neither of us wished for it, but it happened. Let's at least try to keep on with what we've been trying to do this evening.'

He held her eyes for a moment. Hers were not veiled, but what was in them he did not know. Maybe it was simply exhaustion at hearing him out.

Whatever it was, their waiter was now gliding up to their table again, bearing his cheese board and Siena's *tarte*. He set them down, murmuring something about their coffee, and disappeared again.

'That looks good,' Vincenzo said, indicating her dessert.

It seemed a sufficiently neutral comment to make. He followed it with another one.

'In Italy, it's the custom to serve cheese before dessert, rather than after, as in England.'

She picked up her fork. 'Yes, cheese usually rounds off a meal here—unless you count the petit fours or chocolate mints that come with coffee and liqueurs.'

She echoed his neutral, conversational tone, and Vincenzo was glad. He felt in need of it. In need of something simple...easy...

The waiter was approaching again, bearing down on them with their respective coffees. Vincenzo made a start on his cheese. The atmosphere between them had relaxed. Or if not relaxed exactly, it had eased, at least. And he was grateful for it.

For a while there was silence between them, yet it was not a strained one.

We've moved on.

To what, he didn't know. But one thing he did know.

Wherever they'd moved on to, it had to be better than where they'd come from...

That, too, was something to be grateful for.

Siena went on forking up her dessert. Her mood was strange. She tried to find a word for it, but the only one she could come up with was 'exhausted'. Maybe that did sum up the situation. But another one came, too.

Relieved.

She wondered at it for a moment.

Relieved? Did she really feel relieved? And if so, why?

Because we've got something out of the way—something else.

Something other than the apology that she knew must have stuck in his craw.

But he made it all the same.

She frowned inwardly. Yes, he had. She had to give him that. And she had to give him something else—even if it stuck in *her* craw to do so.

He's making an effort.

Because he was—that was obvious.

And I have to as well.

She looked up...looked across at him. His face was unreadable again. Not closed, just...unreadable.

Suddenly, she wanted to read it. 'Were you really shocked that you fell into bed with me like that?'

The words were out of her mouth before she could filter them.

He met her eyes. 'Yes,' he said. 'It's not something I've ever done before.'

She looked puzzled. He had spoken calmly, but she'd picked up something in the timbre of his voice. 'It's not supposed to be something men think is a big deal,' she said slowly. 'Instant sex with a stranger.'

He set down his cheese knife. 'That depends on the man, doesn't it?'

She pondered his answer. Pondered her reaction to it.

She knew that she was if not glad, precisely, at what he'd just said, then she was not the opposite. She also knew she wanted to ask another question—needed to ask it. But it was riskier...much riskier.

'What is it?' he asked. His eyes were still resting on her.

'What's what?' she returned.

'What is it you want to ask me?' he said.

She was taken aback. *How did he know...?*

'Your face is expressive,' he said, as if he'd heard her ask that very question out loud.

There was a touch of dryness in his voice, but it was not harsh, or acerbic. It had the same quality as when he'd said, *'There is no need to beat yourself up about it.'* Then he had touched her cheek...

She swallowed. Her throat had tightened, but she didn't know why.

'If it's a difficult question, I will try to make it easier for you,' he was saying now, and there was still that different timbre to his voice, the new way he was letting his eyes rest on her. She didn't know what it was, but it made her take a breath. Risk asking the question. Blurting it out.

'If...if you hadn't had that early-morning meeting, would you...? Would you have...?'

'Yes,' he said.

She felt her throat untighten—and again she didn't

know why. Only knew that as he went on talking something was changing.

'I would have been tempted to stay...to have breakfast with you.'

She heard his words. Heard the note of admission in them. Heard him continue.

'I don't know what would have happened had I not left as precipitately as I did.'

'Well, we'll never know now, will we?' she said.

'You're right. We'll never know, either of us, what might have come of that night together had I not walked out on you that morning...had you not found yourself pregnant. Which is why we can only deal with the situation as it is—not as it might have been, or might not have been. So...' he drew a breath '...here we are. Trying to find a way forward that is more viable than perhaps either of us thought at first, with my accusations and your anger.'

'I suppose we are,' she said slowly.

She picked up her spoon, absently started to stir the coffee in her cup. Decaf wasn't very appetising, but she took a mouthful anyway. Thoughts were going through her, and what might be emotions or might not—she wasn't sure. She wasn't sure of anything...

He said he might have stayed—at least for breakfast. He'd acknowledged what had happened between them. Acknowledged the night before and the morning after.

That was something. Maybe...

She realised he was talking again, and made herself focus.

'I was thinking...' he was saying, and she could hear the note of reserve in his voice, see the watchfulness in his eyes. 'Perhaps our next step should be to spend some time away. A few days together.'

She stared.

'Somewhere out of London,' he went on. He paused. 'Would you consider that?'

'I don't know,' she said slowly.

Could she cope with spending that kind of time with him?

'There is no rush to decide. I have to return to Italy tomorrow, and then I am in Geneva, and then Turin. But after that… Well, that might be a good time, if it's something you decide to do. Why not give some thought to where might be a good location?'

He left it at that, went back to eating his cheese and biscuits, and she went back to finishing her dessert. They didn't speak, but for the first time the silence didn't seem palpable.

She pushed her empty plate away, drained her unappetising coffee.

'Would you like a refill?' Vincenzo asked.

She shook her head. 'I'll have a fruit tea at the apartment. That way I won't miss the caffeine,' she said.

There was a rueful note in her voice, but it was only lightly rueful.

'Then shall I call for the bill?' he checked.

She nodded, and he summoned their waiter. The waiter came immediately, even though the restaurant had filled up and he was in demand. But then, she thought, Vincenzo Giansante was the kind of man who got waiters' attention whenever he wanted it. Or his wealth got it…

But he hadn't always been wealthy, had he? He'd said he'd made his money from scratch. So maybe there was a time when he couldn't just click his fingers and have waiters come running.

And there was also a thought in her head, disquieting and disturbing, that maybe there had been a time when he didn't have to be suspicious that any female interest in him was influenced by his wealth...

Like wanting to get pregnant by him.

He was putting away his fancy-looking credit card, getting to his feet. She did likewise. They fell into step as they headed back towards the apartment. The night air was cool, and she gave a slight shiver. A moment later he was draping his jacket around her shoulders.

'Oh!' she exclaimed, taken aback. Then: 'Thank you,' she said awkwardly.

It would be ungracious to divest herself of it—and besides, the warmth was welcome.

His body warmth...

It was a disturbing consciousness. Evoking memories...

They didn't speak as they walked—but, again, it was not a tension-filled silence.

At the entrance to the apartment block he stopped. '*Mi dispiace*, but I must relieve you of my jacket. My key is in the pocket.'

'Oh...oh, yes...'

Siena slipped the jacket from her, felt the beautiful soft silk lining sliding over her shoulders. Vincenzo took it from her, fetched out his key, and opened the door into the lobby.

'I'll see you to your door, then bid you goodnight,' he said.

And he did just that, ushering her into the lift, and

then out again, and on to the apartment. By then she'd got her own key out of her handbag, and she used it to open the front door. Then she turned.

In the low light of the landing he seemed very tall, his face half shadowed, his profile thrown into relief. She felt something go through her, but she didn't know what it was.

Didn't want to know.

Because it's not relevant. Not any more. Nor is it appropriate.

'Thank you for dinner,' she said, self-conscious suddenly.

He'd shrugged himself back into his jacket as she'd opened her apartment door. His eyes were resting on her. In the dim light she could not make out his expression. But perhaps that was just as well.

'I think the evening did some good,' he said. 'I will leave you now. You have my contact details, should you need anything, otherwise I will be in touch at the end of next week.' He paused. 'I would ask you to consider what I suggested. See whether you think that our going away together might also do some good?'

She gave a half-nod, not wanting to commit.

'I hope it goes well in Geneva and Turin,' she said instead. It seemed a polite thing to say.

He nodded in the same grave fashion. 'Thank you. And now, *buona notte*.'

'Goodnight,' she echoed, awkward again, and then stepped inside the apartment, closing the door. Shutting him out.

There was a studied expression on her face as she walked into the kitchen. It seemed a long time since she had set off from here earlier in the evening. As if she'd travelled a great distance.

But where she had reached she did not know...

CHAPTER EIGHT

THE SEA WAS a mix of grey and blue. Blue when the intermittent sun came out from behind a scudding cloud, grey when it went behind.

'Would you care to sit down? Are you feeling tired? We've walked some way.' Vincenzo's enquiry was polite.

'Thank you, yes.' Siena's reply was equally polite.

She lowered herself onto the empty bench they had paused beside on the paved promenade. Beyond the railing the tide was in, leaving only a strip of shingle below. Gulls swooped haphazardly, and though the sea breeze was light, white caps dotted the changing surface of the water. Further off shore Vincenzo could see a sailing boat, skimming west to east along the English Channel.

Memory pierced. He'd been watching the yachts off the Sardinian coast, having a leisurely lunch, when that call had come through and had ripped through his life like a cannonball through tissue paper.

And now...

Now he was here, at this genteel seaside resort in east Devon on the coast, sitting beside the woman who had changed his life completely. Changed it irreversibly and for ever.

'Are you warm enough?' he asked her now.

'Thank you, yes,' she said, in the same polite tone.

Politeness was their watchword, and each of them was applying it scrupulously. He was glad of it. Appreciative. They were making progress. But where they were going was still uncertain.

All he could do was keep on in the same direction, glad that she seemed to be acquiescing to his suggestion that they take a break from their lives, have some time away. She had chosen this place—he'd never heard of it—and it seemed acceptable in the circumstances.

'It's supposed to be the prettiest seaside town in Britain,' Siena had told him when she'd let him know that, yes, she would consider his suggestion of getting out of London for a few days.

Overall, Vincenzo felt the description justified. The resort dated, so Siena had told him, to the end of the eighteenth century, when sea bathing was becoming fashionable and resorts were springing up all along the south coast from Brighton to Devon.

Selcombe was small, and all the more charming for it, he thought. He had booked them into the town's main hotel at the far end of the promenade—a handsome white stucco-fronted house, with gardens giving direct access to the shingle beach beyond. Though hardly a luxury hotel, it was comfortable in an old-fashioned way, and he was not displeased with it.

'How are you feeling?' He turned to Siena, sitting beside him—she had left a good space between them, but not pointedly so. 'Can you make it back to the hotel, or shall we take a taxi?'

'Oh, I'm fine,' she answered. 'It's such a lovely day. Let's keep walking—it's only about half a mile, and flat going.' She turned her head to look at him. 'It's really important I keep myself fit, you know.'

'But you must not overdo it,' Vincenzo said.

'A leisurely stroll along a mile of promenade is hardly overdoing it!' There was no sting in her words. 'But it's nice to sit and watch the sea in the sunshine.'

He heard her pause for a moment, as if wondering whether to say what she said next.

'Do you like the seaside? I mean, in Italy? Is it your thing? Some people love the sea…some don't.'

'It's very pleasant,' Vincenzo said.

'Did you go to the seaside when you were young? We lived less than an hour from the coast, and my parents used to take my brother and me to the seaside for the day quite regularly. What about you?'

She was making conversation, he could tell. In principle, he welcomed it, because he was doing likewise. Had been doing so ever since he'd collected her the day previously, in the hire car he'd rented for the week, and headed out of London towards the west country. They had been civil to each other the whole time…polite, pleasant.

And guarded, too, he knew. Both himself and her.

That aspect rose to the fore now.

'No,' he said. He didn't mean to sound curt. 'Milan is not near the coast,' he went on.

'I suppose not,' she said, her gaze going back out over the sea beyond the railings at the edge of the promenade. 'But isn't it close to the Italian lakes?'

'Lake Como is the closest.'

He never went near Como—too many bad associations…

'Did you go as a child? I don't know whether one can swim in the Italian lakes… Not like at the seaside.'

'No,' he said again. This time he managed to make his voice sound less curt. 'And, yes, one can swim, but it is not that safe. The lakes are very deep. They are more appropriate for water sports—there is a lot of sailing, windsurfing, motor boats…that sort of thing.'

'Do you indulge?' she asked.

'No.' He paused, his eyes resting on a sailing boat skimming along the horizon. 'I never seem to have time.'

'That's a shame,' he heard her say. 'I've never done anything like that either.'

From nowhere, Vincenzo heard himself say, 'Perhaps we can do it here—go out on the sea. I've seen signs advertising boat tours along the coast. We could take one. Would that appeal?'

He looked at her again, and saw she had turned her head as well.

'It sounds nice,' she said. There was more than politeness in her voice now.

'Good,' he said. 'Perhaps tomorrow…if the weather is kind.'

'Yes, let's,' Siena agreed peaceably.

Almost subliminally, Vincenzo felt his mood improve, felt himself relax. He stretched out his legs, enjoying the sunshine on his face. It was not hot—that would be impossible compared with Italy—but it was warm, and the light breeze was ruffling his hair.

He let his glance go sideways to Siena. She had leant back on the bench, face lifted to the sunshine that had emerged from behind a scudding cloud, and the sunlight played on her face. She was wearing no make-up, but her hair was not confined to its usual ponytail. It was held back by a band, wisping a little in the breeze. Her eyes were closed.

Vincenzo watched her. With part of his mind he was taking in the delicacy of her profile, the sculpture of her cheekbones, the length of her eyelashes, the curve of her lips, the fall of her hair over her shoulders. He felt something stir within him, and knew what it was—knew he must set it aside promptly, immediately.

But her eyes were still closed, her face still lifted to the sunshine. Her features were in repose—exposed to him. He went on looking at her.

Knowing why.

Knowing he should not.

Deliberately, he dragged his gaze downwards. Her pregnancy was still barely visible—only the slightest roundness beneath the cotton sweater she was wearing over slimly cut trousers. But, barely visible though it was, her pregnancy was real. Increasing…

So the kind of thoughts he was having were simply… Impossible.

Necessarily so.

After all, he reminded himself acidly, it was those thoughts—heated to a white-hot temperature—that had led to him sitting here, on a bench on a seaside promenade in Devon, rearranging his entire life on account of having indulged in them.

He frowned. She was looking so entirely different from the way she'd looked that fateful night at the Falcone. Not vamped up in the slightest. So why was he reacting in the same way?

He made himself look back out to sea again. That was better—safer.

Isn't this situation complicated enough, without adding any more into the mix?

The question was entirely rhetorical. The answer was obvious. And besides…

We are finally getting beyond all that ugly hostility, shock and anger. We are finally capable of being civil to each other, dealing with the situation we face in a calm, rational manner. So the very last thing it needs is disturbance.

Whatever his thoughts were when he let his eyes rest on her, he must keep them entirely private. She'd made it crystal-clear she regarded that night as a mistake.

And so do I—of course I do!

Yet even as he said the words inside his head he could hear refutation taking shape. Did he regret that night? Or only the consequences of it?

His thoughts went back to the restaurant on Holland Park Avenue, where she'd asked him whether, had he not had that prearranged business meeting, he'd have stayed with her…at least for breakfast.

What would we have said to each other had I not left her as I did?

Thoughts moved within him, raising more questions than they answered. Distilling down to one.

Would I have still ended up walking away from her? Putting her into a taxi and out of my mind? Going back to the life I lead. Writing off that night simply as a one-off aberration?

His gaze withdrew from the sea, went back to her face. His head turned.

Her eyes were still closed.

Her face was still lifted to the sun.

Still effortlessly beautiful…

* * *

Siena opened her eyes. She wasn't sure why. It had been so peaceful just sitting there, relaxed, her face lifted to the warmth of the sun, hearing the gulls cry and the waves break on the beach below, with the rhythmic sound of the shingle sliding and tumbling.

But for whatever reason she opened her eyes, turned her head slightly.

And then stilled completely.

Vincenzo was looking at her. Right at her.

No veiling, no guarding, no unreadability.

She felt his eyes on hers, holding hers. As if he could see right into her. Shock rippled through her. The last time he'd looked at her like that it had sent her into meltdown, pooling like honey at his feet... Liquid with answering desire...

For a second—just a second—she felt colour start to flare, her pulse surge, her heart thud. Then, with an effort of will, she dragged her gaze away, back to look out over the sea. Then she got to her feet.

'Shall we keep going?' she said brightly. Too brightly, but she didn't care.

She didn't wait for his answer, only started along the promenade in the direction of their hotel at the far end. The equanimity that she had so assiduously striven for ever since Vincenzo had turned up yesterday after lunch and they'd set off for Devon had evaporated like drops of water on a hot stove.

And she knew exactly what fuel that stove had been heated with...

No! Don't go there! Just don't! It's too dangerous, im-

possible, and totally inappropriate... Irrelevant...out of order. Embarrassing.

And embarrassment was the predominant reaction to that moment back there on the bench. Of course it was! What else could it be?

She'd been caught unawares.

So had he.

The words were stinging in her head, making her acknowledge them. Without realising it, she quickened her pace. Then, realising that might be revealing, she slowed again. Vincenzo fell into step beside her. For the first time she was horribly conscious of his physical presence at her side.

Conscious in that way...

No! She crushed the thought out of her head. That burning night had done quite enough damage to her life—the very last thing she must allow was that it should start smouldering again. She had done her best since Vincenzo had reappeared in her life—dear heaven, she had! Had managed to totally blank him in every way except one.

We just need to be civil with each other, that's all. We can afford no disturbances, no disruption, nothing else to cope with...

'Did you want to have lunch somewhere along the way, or back at the hotel?' she asked now, quite deliberately.

Lunch was a neutral topic, a safe one. Vincenzo seemed to agree.

'Shall we see if we spot anywhere likely as we go?' he said. 'And if we don't, we can always eat at the hotel. Dinner last night was perfectly acceptable, but maybe we don't want to eat there all the time. There may be other good restaurants around…cafés, even. That kind of thing for lunch?'

'OK,' Siena agreed.

She cast her eye across the road that ran between the promenade and the row of buildings on the other side. They were, she could see, Regency-style upmarket villas, a long terrace of them, interrupted every now and then by smaller roads leading away from the seafront. Although the upper floors of the former villas might now be apartments—holiday lets, probably, she thought—the ground floors were mostly either eateries or shops.

'What about over there?' Vincenzo said beside her, pointing to a restaurant with seating on the wide pavement, an awning overhead, and hanging baskets of colourful flowers.

'It looks quite Mediterranean,' Siena said.

'So it does—shall we give it a try? See what's on offer?'

There was a crossing nearby, and he ushered her across. The little restaurant did look nice. Quite a few of the tables were occupied, but Vincenzo guided them to one that was empty, and set back a little.

'Will this do?' he asked her politely.

She nodded with a half-smile and sat down. A waitress bustled up, proffering menus and asking cheerfully what they might like to drink. Siena gave her usual order, and Vincenzo ordered a beer. Siena noticed the waitress paying a lot of attention to Vincenzo. But then, a man with Vincenzo's looks would always draw female eyes…

Mine included…

She put the thought away. Been there, done that—and got the *Baby Bump* tee shirt for her pains…

She studied the menu, trying to replace such thoughts, and opted for a chicken and avocado salad. Vincenzo chose the house speciality—crab salad.

The waitress smiled. 'Fresh-caught this morning,' she said encouragingly, before disappearing with clear reluctance.

Vincenzo sat back in his seat, looking out across the road and the promenade beyond.

'I assume this must have been a fishing village originally,' he observed. 'Before it became a seaside resort.'

'Yes, I think so,' Siena said.

It was a good safe topic to discuss, and would help to keep her mind off the things it must be kept off.

All the same, a thought went through her head…

Had it really been wise to do this? Agree to Vincenzo's suggestion that they spend some time together away from London like this? Well, it was too late now. Too late for a whole lot of things in her life…

Including my art degree…again.

But as she responded to Vincenzo's question about the fashion for sea bathing that had emerged in the mid-eighteenth century, leading to Regency resorts like this and any number of others along the Channel coast, she found herself thinking about something else. Found herself wishing she had her sketchpad with her. She would happily sit on a bench on the promenade…do some pencil sketching of the seascape.

The idea was appealing. Maybe she could find some kind of art shop here and buy some basic kit?

'Did they really have those strange caravans drawn

into the sea by horses, so the bathers could walk down the steps right into the sea?' Vincenzo was asking, his voice amused.

'Yes,' said Siena. 'Bathing machines, they were called. I've seen prints and early photos. Women wore massive swimsuits—for want of a better word—that covered them voluminously from head to toe. Rather like a modern burkini, but even more encompassing! But it let them get into the sea, so it was probably worth it.'

'The *cold* sea,' observed Vincenzo.

'Well, a lot colder than the Med, that's for sure!' she said lightly. She gave a wry laugh. 'In England we say "bracing"—which translates as totally freezing!'

He gave a low laugh. It did things to her.

She went on hurriedly, because she must not let that happen. 'I'm wondering whether to be brave enough to go in myself,' she mused. 'The Channel can't be any colder than the North Sea—but then, of course, back then I was a child, and didn't care about cold water! Besides, after a while you warm up.'

He cast a sceptical glance at her.

She gave another wry smile. 'You could always just paddle. You know—take your socks and shoes off, roll up your trouser legs and wade in.' Now her smile turned to a laugh. 'You could also do the time-honoured old-fashioned English thing that men did a couple of generations ago, and that is to take a linen handkerchief, knot it at each corner, and put it on your head.'

He looked at her. 'To what purpose?' he enquired, nonplussed.

'To keep the sun off,' she explained.

'If the sun ever gets that hot, I shall purchase a hat,' he told her decisively.

She laughed again. 'Definitely more stylish. The knotted handkerchief was never a good look!'

'Thank you for the warning,' he said dryly. His mouth quirked. 'And as for paddling... I think I may give that a miss too. The hotel pool will suffice—it is heated.'

'Yes,' she conceded, 'I have to agree it sounds more tempting. But when the tide is out we can walk along the beach, at least. Feel the shingle crunching. It's a shame it's not a sandy beach,' she mused. 'Where we went as a child had a wonderful sandy beach, with dunes behind. My brother and I were delirious, making sandcastles, playing beach cricket, as well as actual sea bathing. My parents would sit on deckchairs, glad just to watch us, and my mother would knit, and my father would read a paperback, and then they'd call us back to them for a picnic lunch. We were always starving by then, and when it was finally time to go home we were treated to ice creams to eat before setting off.'

She realised Vincenzo was looking at her with a strange expression on his face.

'You sound as if you had a happy childhood,' he said slowly.

'I did,' she said. 'Very happy...'

'How old were you,' he asked quietly, 'when your parents were killed?'

'I was eighteen. My brother twenty-three. He'd just qualified as a vet and was newly married, and—'

She broke off. This was painful territory. The attentive waitress bustled back to their table with their drinks, and Siena was glad. She sipped hers thirstily, and Vincenzo took a leisurely mouthful of his beer. She looked away, over the other holidaymakers having their lunch, carefree and happy. Or were they? How could you tell just by looking? After all, who, looking at her and Vincenzo, would know why it was they were there, apparently together, apparently a couple…

When all we have between us is a baby that neither of us planned, envisaged, expected or wanted.

She felt her throat tighten suddenly, and slid her hand over her abdomen. It was rounding more day by day, making its presence felt. Inexorably, unstoppably…

She became aware that Vincenzo was saying something, setting his beer glass back on the table.

'It is hard to lose a parent at any age,' he was saying, and there was a quality to his voice that made Siena look across at him. 'I, too, lost my father at eighteen—a heart attack. My mother died when…'

He paused, and she had the impression he had stopped himself. She looked at him questioningly, sympathy in her eyes.

'She died when I was four,' he said.

'That is very hard,' Siena said slowly.

It seemed strange to think of Vincenzo as a child—as having a family at all. Hadn't he said he had 'none worth mentioning'? But if both his parents were dead…

We have that in common.

It was a painful thing to share…

Vincenzo was frowning. 'I don't have many memories of her. Just one or two. And they may be from my father telling me about her. It's hard to say.'

'Do…do you have any siblings?' Siena heard herself asking. 'For me, it was such a comfort to have my brother, and he to have me,'

Vincenzo gave a shake of his head. His expression had tightened. 'No,' he said. 'Which was one of the reasons why my father—'

He broke off, and Siena looked at him questioningly again.

'Why he wanted to remarry.'

'Did…did he remarry?'

'Eventually.' Vincenzo's voice was even tighter. 'I was thirteen.'

She was feeling her way forward. To hear Vincenzo open up like this was strange…

He wouldn't do it if we weren't in this situation. And nor would I.

But maybe it was important that they were doing so? Knowing more about each other. Coming to terms with each other.

'Did…did you get on with your stepmother?'

Something hardened in his face, making him look the way he had that nightmare day in his office, when she'd blurted out that she was pregnant.

'No.'

A single word. He reached for his beer, took another mouthful. Set down the glass with a click.

'Nor did I ever consider her my stepmother—nor do I still.'

'Still?'

He gave a shrug—a dismissive one. 'She took herself off when my father died…set herself up in a villa on Lake Como.'

Siena spoke slowly, carefully. 'That sounds…expensive.'

Vincenzo's eyes flashed. 'She took my father for everything he had left,' he bit out harshly.

In the silence, things reshaped themselves in Siena's head.

Things were making sense...

Dark and difficult sense—but sense.

So that is why he made all those vile assumptions about me—thinking the worst of me...

Quietly, she spoke again, wanting him to hear—wanting him to believe. 'I'm not like that,' she said. Her voice was low, intense.

For a long moment—dark and difficult—his eyes held hers. She could feel her heart beating in her breast as she went on holding his eyes still.

Suddenly, his lashes swept down over his eyes, shutting her out, cutting off the moment. Then they opened again. His expression had changed, and Siena felt her stretched nerves ease. A half-smile, twisted, pulled at Vincenzo's mouth, as if in acknowledgement of what she had said.

'I should not need you to say it,' he said.

'No,' she agreed, still meeting his eyes, 'but perhaps it helps all the same...'

He gave a nod. 'Perhaps it does,' he echoed.

He glanced away for a moment, out over the promenade across the road, then looked back at Siena. The wry expression in his face was there again.

'We have moved on again,' he said.

He was making his voice light, she could hear it, and she answered him in the same fashion. Wanting to for her own sake—and for his.

'Yes,' she said.

She reached for her own drink and took a draught, her mouth dry.

The arrival of their salads was timely, giving respite from what had been said…revealed. They were huge—Vincenzo's laden with flaked crab meat.

'Enjoy,' said their waitress, casting a look at Vincenzo.

He gave her a polite nod of thanks, but nothing more, and with her sigh almost audible the waitress headed away.

The waitress's were not the only female eyes to be lingering on Vincenzo, Siena could see. At least two other women sitting nearby were throwing him covert glances.

It was totally obvious why. The combination of his lethal looks, fatally augmented by his Mediterranean aura, made it impossible for anyone in possession of a double X chromosome to be unaware of him.

She let her eyes rest on him for a moment as he got stuck into his crab salad. He was casually dressed, but the style and expense of his clothes was unmistakable. The open-necked polo shirt bore a designer mark on the breast pocket that she vaguely recognised as that of a top Milan fashion house. It was worn with superbly cut but casually styled chinos, and rounded off with an even more beautifully cut and styled dressed-down jacket.

He looked cool, Italian—and devastating.

She gave a silent gulp, bending her attentions to her own salad.

Casting about for a safe subject, wanting an easier topic of conversation—less intense, less dark and difficult—she said, 'I wonder if Lyme Regis is very far. It would be worth seeing. The harbour has a high, protective breakwater called the Cob, made famous by Jane Austen,' she said.

Vincenzo raised a querying eyebrow.

Siena elaborated. 'She set a key scene there in *Persuasion*, her last novel. The heroine's sister-in-law, whom the heroine fears is going to marry the man she herself loves, but who no longer loves her, impulsively jumps down from the steps on the upper Cob to the lower and is nearly fatally injured.'

'Only nearly? No tragic ending, then?' he said sardonically.

'No, it's all right. The rival to the heroine does make a full recovery, but she falls for one of the hero's friends and marries him instead, so the hero is free to realise he loves the heroine after all, and they get their happy-ever-after.'

'That is reassuring,' observed Vincenzo. 'At least in novels there can be good resolution of life's problems.' Siena heard his voice change. 'Perhaps we must strive to do likewise in our lives too,' he said. 'Even when those problems seem…intractable.'

His eyes rested on her. His expression was grave.

'I appreciate, Siena, all that you are doing. Truly I do. You are meeting me halfway, and I hope I am doing the same.' He paused for a moment. 'Do you think this is helping? Time together like this?'

She met his gaze, and there was honesty in hers. 'Yes. It's strange—it can't be anything *but* strange. But, yes, I think it is helping.'

But helping us to do what? Helping us be civil to each other, yes—and to understand each other more, to see where we are coming from, each of us. But it can't change anything else. I still wish I had not got pregnant.

And, given that I am, I still want to move somewhere on my own to have my baby, not be dependent on Vincenzo.

Her thoughts were turbid. If he could finally believe she wasn't interested in his money, now that she understood where that fear had come from—*that I might be like his father's second wife*—couldn't he accept her making a home for herself and the baby? If he wanted, he could visit from time to time—set up a trust fund or whatever, if he felt that was his responsibility. Wouldn't that be more feasible, now that they were not at war any longer?

She broke her gaze, letting it go back out over the bustling promenade. She was very conscious of Vincenzo's presence so close across the table. Conscious, too, that there was another reason other than her being independent for not giving him any grounds to think she was after his money, for why she wanted him at a distance once the baby arrived.

Because anything else is dangerous...

She felt her gaze wanting to return to his face, and that was proof itself of the danger she felt flickering around her.

He was dangerous to me that night at the Falcone— disastrously so. And for all that the hostility and accusations between us are gone, that danger is still there.

Lethal. That was what Megan had called his darkly handsome looks—and it was an apt word. Didn't just sitting here having lunch with him demonstrate that, with every female around turning their heads just because he was there?

I have to keep myself safe from him, safe from the danger he is to me...to my heart. It's not as though he would ever truly see a future with someone like me—if he sees a future with anyone at all. So it's safest, surely, just to focus on what we are doing now—getting used to each other, letting there be some kind of peace between us. Asking nothing more than that. Wanting nothing more than that... Not letting myself want more.

Because that would only spell danger.

She gave a silent sigh. Life was already far too complicated to allow anything more into it. All she must focus on was the baby—nothing else.

Nothing else at all...

Least of all the man she had been unable to resist that fateful night, who had brought her to the now she had to deal with.

CHAPTER NINE

LYME REGIS WAS just as Siena had said. They walked along the Cobb, with Siena pointing out the steps that featured so dramatically in the Jane Austen novel. Out at the far end the sea breeze was stronger, buffeting them both. Vincenzo put his arm around Siena's shoulder to steady her. He'd made the gesture without thinking about it, but the moment he did he almost drew back. She'd stiffened, tensed.

'I don't want you blown into the sea,' he said.

'It is definitely windier here,' she allowed.

He felt the tension in her shoulders subside fractionally. All the same, as soon as the gust passed he lowered his arm.

They stood awhile, braced against the buffeting wind, watching it whipping up the water. The sun was bright, turning the sea to scintillating diamonds.

'We could take another boat trip if you like,' Vincenzo said.

They'd done so a few days ago, cruising sedately along the shoreline and back again. It had been pleasant, sitting against the gunwale, watching the other passengers taking photographs of the shore passing them by.

'It looks a bit too bumpy today,' Siena said. 'That's quite a strong swell. I think.'

'Then we shall pass,' Vincenzo said. 'Perhaps we could try our hand at fossil-hunting after lunch?' he asked. Fossils, he had learnt, were something Lyme Regis was famous for.

'That might be fun,' Siena said.

She was still being careful with him, Vincenzo could tell. But then he was being careful with her. Scrupulously polite, courteously conversational.

They stepped off the Cobb and headed towards the town, choosing a pub that served fresh-caught fish for lunch, eating indoors this time, as the wind was so brisk. The low-pitched, smoke-darkened beams were atmospheric, and although the place was designed to cater for tourists, the fresh fish was indeed very tasty.

Afterwards they ventured along the start of the Under-cliff, having purchased a guide to Lyme's fossils from a handy souvenir shop. The raised beach was strewn with boulders, and difficult walking terrain, so Vincenzo kept his eyes fixed on Siena, who took her steps carefully. They spotted a large rounded rock, suitable for perching, and did so. Vincenzo opened the fossil guide and they discussed the fossils the place was famous for, and what might yet be found.

'As it's called the Ammonite Pavement,' Siena commented, 'I guess that's what we'll see most of.'

It was—and quite spectacularly so.

'It makes one realise,' Vincenzo said slowly, 'how brief a span of time we occupy on this earth...how short a lifetime is...'

She was silent a moment. Then: 'Some are very short indeed…'

He could hear a strange note in her voice—something that made him look at her.

'What is it?' he asked quietly.

But she only shook her head and changed the subject.

They went on, strolling carefully, but not going too far, before turning and retracing their steps. There were plenty of other fossil-hunters along the way, or just walkers—a good few with dogs in tow. One dog—a large one, rushing around off its leash—came bounding up to them, jumping at Siena.

Vincenzo thrust it away ungently, speaking sharply to him in Italian. The dog gave a bark and bounded away again.

'Are you all right?' Vincenzo asked Siena.

She looked a little shaken, for the dog had been large, and had taken her by surprise.

'Yes, fine… I think he was more friendly than anything.'

'Uncontrolled,' said Vincenzo sternly.

The dog was careering towards them again, clearly over-excited. As it approached, Vincenzo held out an arm, simultaneously warding it off Siena and giving it another order in Italian. The dog stopped, then sniffed at his outstretched hand. It gave another bark. Then licked Vincenzo's hand and bounded off, hearing its owner calling belatedly to it.

The woman came up to them. 'He's just being friendly,' she said.

'But not everyone loves dogs,' Vincenzo pointed out severely. 'And you—' he addressed the dog directly now, which was licking his still outstretched hand again '—are a fearsome beast!' His voice was severe but the dog knew perfectly well that he was being praised, and barked happily again.

Siena, beside him, held out her own hand for him to sniff. 'But no jumping!' she admonished.

The fearsome beast's owner smiled apologetically. 'I'm sorry...he does get over-enthusiastic. But he mustn't jump up, I know—especially when you are in your condition.' She smiled again. 'When's it due?'

Siena looked taken aback.

'I'm a midwife,' the woman said with another smile. 'I'd say...' she cast a professional eye at Siena '...you're around sixteen weeks.'

'Seventeen,' confirmed Siena.

The woman's smile broadened—her dog had gone bounding away over the beach now, clearly done with them.

'Your first? How wonderful for you both! You must be so happy and excited! I know it will seem like ages and ages yet, but believe me...' her voice warmed '...when it finally happens you'll both be over the moon. I promise!' Her smile included them both. 'I wish you all the very best—this is such a special time of your lives, so enjoy every moment!'

'Thank you,' said Vincenzo with difficulty.

Siena said nothing.

The woman moved to go, pausing only to say, 'I'll keep my dog well away from you, but do take care on this stony beach. You really don't want to trip and fall at this stage.' She smiled again one last time. 'And congratulations!' she said warmly.

She walked away, calling to her dog. For a moment there was only silence between him and Siena. His eyes went to her. There was an expression on her face he had not seen before.

'I guess to others it does look like that,' she said, and he could hear the strain in her voice. 'As if we're just a normal couple starting a family. When we're not even a couple. And a family is the last thing we'll ever be.'

She started to walk, picking her steps carefully. Her shoulders seemed to be hunched, Vincenzo thought.

There was a tightness in his chest as he walked after her and his eyes followed her—the woman who had in one fateful moment, on one fateful night, set him aflame with something he had never felt before. Something for which he had no explanation, no excuse, no exoneration, but which had consumed him with its intensity.

It should never have happened—it had been insane self-indulgence—but he'd gone for it all the same, taking his fill, yielding to the flame she'd lit in him. Burning in it.

He'd kept that woman ruthlessly away from the one now walking away from him. Locked her away in the past, to that single night.

He quickened his pace. That woman's voice—the midwife's—in his head now, warning that Siena should not stumble or trip.

Siena who had ignited that flame in him and Siena who was pregnant with their child.

He did not allow them to be the same person. How could they be?

Once so physically intimate—yet a stranger.

But now?

No physical intimacy—nothing of that burning flame could exist—yet no longer a stranger.

So who is she to me?

The question hung in his head. He should answer it, but he had no answer to give.

Siena was sitting at a little ironwork table, sketchbook propped up, watercolour pencils to hand, newly purchased that morning. Her gaze was going from the view of the hotel's gardens and the sea beyond to what she was capturing of both on paper.

Vincenzo was in his room, touching base with his office, catching up with his affairs. They'd been here nearly a week now. The days were slipping by, undemanding and unhurried, as they toured around, sightseeing and exploring the lush Devon and Dorset countryside and the scenic coastline.

Day by day it was becoming easier between them, Siena acknowledged. So their time here was achieving its purpose. Defusing the toxic hostility that had been so destructive.

She was still conscious of the tension within her, though. Of her continual awareness of Vincenzo...of what he could arouse in her—which she must not allow. She suppressed it as much as she could, but it was there all the same, all the time...

She dipped the nib of her pencil in the water jar, refocussing on her sketching, pulling her thoughts back to safer ground. It was good to be working again. OK, it wasn't the kind of testing artwork she'd have been striving for at art school, but it was enjoyable enough.

The familiar stab of regret, that being pregnant had

destroyed her hopes of finally getting to art school a second time around, came now. She pushed it away—because what was the point of dwelling on what could not be? Reached instead for a deep crimson, ideal for a splash of flowers in the foreground.

'That's very good.'

Vincenzo's deep, accented voice behind her made her start.

She turned her head.

And gulped silently.

The sunshine was bright—bright enough for Vincenzo to be sporting shades. She gulped again. Oh, good grief! What *was* it about men and sunglasses? They could turn the most unprepossessing male into someone to look twice at. But when sunglasses adorned a man like Vincenzo...

She crushed her reaction down. She could allow it no place.

Belatedly, she realised he'd spoken to her. 'Oh, thank you,' she said, hoping her voice was normal.

He was standing behind her, looking down at her sketch. 'It *is* good,' he said again. 'There's a talent there you should not ignore.'

Siena gave a flickering smile. It was an awkward subject.

'I enjoy it,' she said. 'But that's all.'

He gave a quick shake of his head. 'Talent should always be developed,' he said. His gaze rested on her speculatively.

'You've never really told me about yourself—what you've done with your life so far. Can it be that it's this?'

There was a quizzical note in his voice now, and he gestured towards her sketchbook.

She took a breath. Why make a secret of it? Once she'd have said it was none of his business—that she didn't want him knowing anything about her because she didn't want anything to do with him ever again, after the way he'd treated her. But now—well, there was no reason not to tell him.

'I was going to study art,' she said. 'In fact, the reason I was in London, staying with Megan, was because...' She took another breath. 'I was going to start an art degree this autumn. Obviously because of the baby that's all gone now...' An edge slid into her voice that she could not stop, and she gave a shrug. 'But I'll survive. I gave up on it once before—'

She stopped abruptly.

'Why was that?' Vincenzo was asking frowningly.

But that was a place she did not want to go...

Too painful.

She got to her feet, packing away her pencils, emptying the water jar on the grass, picking up her sketchpad. 'I'll finish this off later,' she said. 'Isn't it time for lunch?'

She was glad he followed her lead—grateful. He got to his feet again, fell into step beside her as they headed indoors.

'Did you have a productive morning?' she asked, conscious that her voice was too bright.

He took her cue, and she was glad of that too.

'Thank you, yes. I can be clear now for a while. Tell me...what might you like to do this afternoon?'

They settled on an excursion further west along the coastline, meandering along country lanes, stopping for a cream tea at a pretty thatched olde-worlde teashop nestled in a sheltered valley, with glorious views over the sparkling English Channel. It was leisurely, undemanding, like all their days.

Serving the purpose for which they were here, Siena acknowledged. To come to terms—civil, unhostile terms—with the situation in which they both unwillingly found themselves.

No other reason.

Her eyes went to him now, as they headed back in the late afternoon. His focus was on the winding road as he drove, strong hands curved around the driving wheel, his face in profile.

But what if there were another reason they were here like this?

What if we were here together because we wanted to be with each other? Just Vincenzo and me, without a baby to complicate everything between us. What if we hadn't met at that party, with me dressed to kill and all that instant heat between us? What if we'd got to know each other slowly—taken things at a slower pace—romanced each other gradually? Spent time with each other the way we're doing now? Got to know each other first, without falling into bed so fast, the way we did...?

But it hadn't happened like that, had it?

She felt something tug at her inside, wanting admission.

She pulled her gaze away, moved it back over the passing countryside.

She felt a heaviness within her.

A sense of loss for what had never been. Never could be now.

I am here with him only because I am pregnant with his baby.

Anything else had been.

And gone.

Vincenzo eased back on the accelerator—these winding West Country roads were not designed for speed, with their thick hedgerows and blind corners. But the landscape was highly appealing, lushly green and rolling, with sheep and cattle placid and contented, the villages quaint and picturesque.

Touring around, sightseeing like this all week, had been very pleasant.

And it had achieved its purpose.

He flicked his glance to Siena, sitting beside him. She was gazing out of the window, an abstracted quality about her. She looked effortlessly lovely...

For a second he let his gaze linger, before returning it to the winding road. But his thoughts stayed with her. What was it about her that made him want to look at her the way he did? He had known beautiful women before, but with Siena there was something...

Something that wasn't just the way she'd looked that night at the Falcone.

Something that drew his eyes to her even as she was now, her hair held back by a simple band, wearing a short-sleeved cotton shirt and loose cropped cotton trousers, not a scrap of make-up, doing nothing to adorn herself. But there was a beauty to her, a glow about her, that made him want to turn his head again.

Perhaps it's pregnancy that makes her bloom?

If it was, then he welcomed it.

He drew his thoughts up short. Decided to speak instead. On a safer subject.

'Shall we dine at the hotel tonight?' he asked conversationally. 'I understand there's a special tasting menu, provided by assorted local producers to showcase their offerings. It's something of an occasion. What do you think?'

He glanced at her again. That abstracted quality had vanished, and she had turned towards him.

'I think it sounds good,' she replied. 'Does it require dressing up?'

'Nothing formal—just smart casual, I would think. I won't wear a tie.'

'Well, I think I've got something that will do, then,' she answered. 'There was a little charity shop next to where I bought my art materials this morning, and there was a summery dress in the window for only a fiver. It's got a loosely elasticated waist, so it will give as I get bigger.'

'That sounds just right,' he approved.

He had spoken politely, but he was conscious that he would like to see Siena in something more beguiling than her habitual tops and trousers. And he was conscious of why...

He pulled his thoughts and his glance away.

Refocussed on his driving and on his reason for being here with Siena. The only reason he should admit to.

As the mother of my child. Only that...

Yet even as he said the words to himself he knew that with every passing day it was not the only truth.

It is for herself...

* * *

'Thank you—but only a little.' Vincenzo held his hand up decisively.

The rep from the cider farm smiled encouragingly and poured some of the amber coloured apple brandy she was tempting diners with after their meal.

'Do try,' she said hopefully, clearly wanting him to take a taste while she was hovering.

He did so, and the spirit bit at the back of his throat. He dared not think what proof it was, but it was strong.

'It's very good,' he said to the rep, and she beamed.

'It's ten years old and matured in cognac barrels,' she said. 'Bottles are available in the lobby if you are interested.'

'I will consider it,' he said gravely.

The rep smiled, then turned her attention to Siena. 'What about you?' she said hopefully.

'Alas, no alcohol at all for me,' said Siena ruefully.

'What a shame,' the rep said, and regretfully abandoned them for another table.

Siena looked across at him. 'What's it like? I don't think I've ever heard of apple brandy before.'

'Strong,' said Vincenzo. 'And, yes, very good. But...' he made a slight face '...so many of the producers here seem to feature alcohol!'

'Devon is famous for cider,' Siena told him. 'But wine production is newer. I would have happily tried that white wine you had earlier. Though my blackberry crémant was very good. And I'm definitely tempted by the blackberry vinegar that was in the *jus* accompanying my lamb, which was also very good. In fact, I don't know about you, but I thought all the dishes were really good! Of course, I don't have your gourmet palette, but I do hope you didn't think the menu beneath you.'

'On the contrary,' Vincenzo assured her.

He meant it too. The tasting menu had been varied, and inventive, and a good showcase for local producers. The dining room was full, and dinner was not yet over. Another rep came by, this time with a tray of handmade chocolate truffles.

'Ah, those I can indulge in!' Siena said happily, and took two, promising the rep that she would certainly be buying a box for herself.

Vincenzo sat back with his glass of apple brandy, his gaze resting on her as she bit into the luscious-looking truffle, her eyes half closing in appreciation. He let his gaze linger. He had, he knew, imbibed more alcohol than he would normally have drunk over dinner, but it had seemed churlish to refuse the plentiful offerings—from a gin cocktail infused with countryside botanicals, through to a really very palatable English vineyard dry white wine with the meal, followed by a very good, sweet dessert wine, and now by the simultaneously fiery but mellowing—and indeed very strong—apple-brandy.

The effect was lowering his guard.

And that was dangerous.

He felt his eyes drift over Siena's face. Memory came, infusing the present with the past.

The dangerous past.

The *very* dangerous past.

The past that had brought him to this very moment, sitting opposite her in this Devonshire hotel, late in the evening, after a leisurely dinner, comfortable and replete, his appetites sated.

Except for one appetite.

An appetite he could feel rising within him. Welling up in him, reaching out into his limbs, his whole body.

He let his gaze rest on her. The dress she was wearing, which she'd told him she'd bought in a charity shop, might not be a designer number like the one she'd worn that night at the Falcone, but it was every bit as effective. With a scooped neckline and cap sleeves, worn with a lacy wrap around her shoulders, it had a blue floral print that brought out the haunting colour of her deep-set eyes, the long lashes dipping on her silky skin. She'd left her hair loose, fastened at each side with a small clip, exposing the tender lobes of her ears.

He took another slow mouthful of apple brandy, letting it warm his blood. His eyelids drooped, his gaze resting on her as he leant back in his chair, fingers curved around his glass.

Looking at her...

Desiring her...

He should not let himself...should not indulge himself. Should straighten, look away, make some anodyne remark to break the moment.

But he did not.

He tried to think of all the reasons why he should keep his guard high—all the reasons that had pressed upon him every time he'd caught himself looking at her, remembering that searing night he'd spent with her. They were good reasons—he knew they were. His brain knew them at any rate.

Because the situation between us is complicated—uncertain—unprecedented. Because so much is at stake and I have to tread carefully, watching each step.

But right now he didn't want to think of all that. He wanted only to go on doing what he was doing, letting his gaze rest on her, absorb her, linger on her...

His gaze dipped to her neckline. It was hardly a dramatic decolletage, but for all that it shaped the swell of her breasts...breasts that were now more generous. His eyes narrowed infinitesimally as he took another slow, leisurely mouthful of the potent apple brandy. Her whole body was more generous too, rounding and ripening. Making her even more beautiful than ever...

He felt desire rise within him, quicken in his heated blood.

She swallowed her truffle, opened her eyes.

Looked straight into his...

CHAPTER TEN

WEAKNESS WASHED THROUGH HER. It was as if every bone in her body were dissolving...as if the room around them were vanishing...the whole world vanishing...evaporating...and all that existed was Vincenzo's gaze on her...consuming her.

Memory flared, hot and instant, sending colour coursing into her cheeks, then draining it from them just as swiftly.

He had looked at her like that before, with those long-lashed, hooded eyes of his, so dark, so impenetrable, yet with an open message in them that had made her very bones, then as now, dissolve... He'd looked at her as they had finally finished dinner that night at the Falcone, *knowing* there was only one way the evening was going to end...and that end was coming. Coming as he had got to his feet, his eyes never leaving her, their sensual glance weakening her, so that when he'd held out his hand to her she had put hers into his, and he'd drawn her to her feet, and she had gone with him...

And now it was happening again...

She felt the fatal weakness wash through her, more dissolving still...

She must fight it. Surely she must give it no room, no space. She must deny it...resist it. Because how could she not? How could she let happen again what had happened before? She must reject it…find the strength to do so.

But she had no strength—none…

His lidded gaze was on her still, holding hers, and heat flushed through her still. She was helpless to pull her eyes away. Quite helpless…

A voice beside her spoke. 'May I offer you some coffee?'

It was one of the waitresses, coffee jug in hand, smiling politely at her.

Siena turned her head, clutched at the lifeline.

'Oh…er…um, have you got tea instead?' she asked. 'A mint tea?'

Did she sound breathless? She must, surely. She fought for composure, to beat down the flaring of heat inside her.

'Of course.' The waitress smiled. Then turned her attention to Vincenzo. 'Coffee for you, sir?' she enquired.

'Thank you,' he answered.

His voice was mechanical, Siena could tell. But his gaze—his disastrous, dissolving gaze—had been switched off. She realised her heart was beating in an agitated manner, and sought to subdue it, to subdue the colour flushing in and out of her cheeks.

The waitress poured coffee into Vincenzo's cup, offered milk, which was refused, then promised Siena she would return with her mint tea. She moved off to the next table.

Urgently, Siena cast about for a safe thing to say, to take them away from the moment that had been so dangerous…

No, don't think it—don't allow it in—don't even think about thinking it. Just go... Before it's too late...

She felt herself get to her feet. 'I think I'll pass on the mint tea after all,' she said. 'It's been a long day. I'll head up to bed. Enjoy the rest of your apple brandy. Thank you for dinner.'

Her voice was staccato, and she knew it, but it was the best she could do.

With a smile that took more effort than she'd thought she was capable of she turned away, heading towards the dining room doors, walking rapidly, wanting only to get away...

Because she must.

Because anything else was too dangerous...

Far, far too dangerous.

But even as she fled, footsteps came after her.

Vincenzo had knocked back the last of his apple brandy and got to his feet, and now he strode after her. She'd paused by the lift, and his eyes went to her. She was running from him—and he did not want her to.

Silhouetted against the metallic doors of the lift, she was more beautiful than ever, with her long hair curving over her shoulders, the lacy fall of her wrap, the soft drape of her summer dress, her slender calves, bared arms...

So beautiful...

He felt the breath tighten in his lungs as he came up to her. She started at his approach, her head turning swiftly to him, eyes flaring.

'Let me see you to your room,' he said.

He could hear a husk in his voice...knew why. She

looked up at him. Her eyes were wide, and in them was apprehension—and something else entirely.

'No…no, it's fine…really…'

He ignored her. The lift doors were opening and she stepped inside. He followed her. He could feel his heart thudding in his chest. He stabbed the button for their floor. His room was at the far end of the corridor, but hers was closer to where the lift disgorged them, and as she walked to her door, her gait quickening, fumbling for the key in her handbag, he closed in on her.

He did not speak. Then, as she turned the old-fashioned key in the lock, he said her name, his voice more husky yet.

She turned, lifting her face to him. Her eyes were wide. Pupils dilated.

'Vincenzo…' Her voice was faint, so faint. 'No—we can't…we mustn't…'

He took no notice. And as her hand pushed open the door, he reached out his hand to her…

She had no breath in her body—none. His hand was curving around the nape of her neck. He said her name. Low and husked. She saw his eyelids dip down over his eyes, watched him lowering his mouth to hers.

It was velvet on her lips…soft, infinitely seductive… and as his mouth moved on hers he pulled her to him, drawing her inside her room. A thousand sensations blinded her as he shut the door behind them. A low, helpless moan came from her, and she felt her limbs dissolving as the velvet of his mouth weakened everything about her. Her hands went around him, to hold and support her, for she had no strength at all. The hard wall of his chest pressed against her breasts, and she felt, with a dim sense of helpless fatality, how they engorged and flowered...

Another moan came from her and her mouth opened to his as his kiss deepened, her hands winding around him, holding him against her. He said something to her, low and husky in his native language. A kind of madness was coming over her, and as he scooped her up into his arms she let him do so. The room had disappeared, the world had disappeared, the whole universe had disappeared. There was only this...only now...only Vincenzo. He was carrying her to her bed, lowering her down upon it, coming down beside her, his mouth never leaving hers.

She was in meltdown—she knew she was. It was as if she had been taken to another existence, one in which only the sweet bliss of *now* was real. For bliss it was, and sweet it was, and all that she craved...

Somewhere, dimly, in what was left of her consciousness, she knew that this time with Vincenzo was far different from the way it had been before. Then it had been an urgent, burning flame, fierce, white-hot, incandescent, sensual, ecstatic, with each of them feeding upon the other, hungry for each other, unleashed upon each other. There had been no time for anything else. Desire— raw, visceral, physical desire—had burned, had blazed between them, wreathing them in its flames, stripping the clothes from their bodies, making them uninhibited, greedy for the sensations that naked intimacy aroused between them, their bodies winding around each other, flexing and writhing, feasting wantonly and wildly.

Now there was no wildness, no hungry urgency. Now

there was a slow, sensuous coming together, with each touch of his lips, his fingers, his tongue, his palms, celebrating the beauty of her body—a body that ripened under his as his hands splayed out over her abdomen, smoothing its soft roundness. His mouth lowered to trace its gentle contours, softly and sensuously. Then his hands were lifting to her breasts, filling his curving palms.

She felt her limbs loosen, his body moving over hers. And in the darkened room, their clothes long shed, she gave herself to him, taking him in return, his long, lean body covering hers, hers yielding to his. They did not speak, and yet she heard soft murmurous Italian from him as his mouth kissed her breasts, her throat, her lips. His kisses were deep, impassioned, yet without frenzied urgency, only with slow, sweet bliss. A bliss he drew from her as he moved his body within hers, setting not a raging fire but a low, warm flame, melting and dissolving her, fusing her to him and him to her.

And when her moment came, it was a warmth, a sweet, liquid pleasure, that spread from her very core to every cell in her body, even to the tips of her fingers, with a honeyed glow that made her cry out softly…so softly… her body lifting to his, her hands pressing the sculpted contours of his back to hold him close, so close…

She felt him surge within her, felt her own body flex and pulse, drawing him in yet deeper, fusing with him, becoming one with him, as still her own moment went on and endlessly on.

And when it finally ebbed, tears were wet upon her cheeks.

Tears for so, so much…

* * *

Vincenzo stirred, sleep gradually leaving him, consciousness gradually returning. Daylight was filling the room—the curtains were undrawn since the night before. His arm reached out across the double bed.

The empty double bed.

Instantly, he was fully awake, his eyes searching the room. The empty room. The door to the en suite bathroom stood open.

The empty en suite bathroom.

He swung himself out of bed.

'Siena?' His voice was sharp, urgent.

No answer came.

No answer was going to come.

Siena had gone.

He slumped back against the pillows, staring out into the room. Heart thudding.

He heard his phone—still in the pocket of his discarded jacket, dropped somewhere on the floor near the bed. Instantly he went to it, snatched it up. A text—from Siena.

He read it, and frowned, then dropped the phone on the tangled bedclothes. But the words in the text were crystal-clear in his head.

I can't do this. I can't do any of it. I'm sorry—I just can't. I'm sorry.

Siena sat in the railway carriage, heading back to London. Words were going over and over in her head, in rhythm with the wheels of the train over the track.

I'm sorry... I'm sorry... I'm sorry.

It was all that was in her head. All that she would allow. All that she dared allow.

She urged the train onwards. She had to get to London before Vincenzo could. Had to get to the apartment he'd taken for her. Had to get there, pack her necessities, and get out. The holiday clothes she'd taken to the seaside would have to be packed by one of the hotel maids, unless Vincenzo did it. And either he would bring her small suitcase with him, her newly purchased sketchbook and pencils, or have it sent on to her.

Wherever she was.

But where would that be?

Into her head a new question formed, repeating over the relentless sound of the train wheels.

Where can I go? Where can I go? Where can I go?

She did not know. Not yet. But she must think of somewhere. She must.

She *must*...

Vincenzo was in Milan. He might as well be. There was no point being in England. Not any more. Siena had made that clear. Crystal-clear. He knew where she was, and for now that must do. He was not out of touch with her—not completely. She sent him brief monthly updates, reports from the midwife appointments she went to. Her pregnancy was progressing healthily—that was all he knew.

He knew he must allow her this. Allow her time and space and distance.

Because she does not want anything more from me.

He felt emotion stab at him, but he crushed it back down. There was no point allowing it...permitting it.

I have to accept that she wants nothing more than what she has made clear—completely clear.

And he must respect that—he had no choice but to do so. All he could do was what he was doing now. Leave her be.

The way she wanted.

Until…

When her time comes I shall be there. Be there for her.

On that he would insist.

CHAPTER ELEVEN

SIENA WAS WASHING UP, looking out of the kitchen window into the garden at the back of the little terraced house. In the summer it was a holiday let, but she had rented it for the winter. In the garden, a robin and a blackbird were hopping about. She must put out some more food for them.

She moved slowly towards the back door that opened on to the garden. Her gait was ponderous now…gravid. Her feet had disappeared from view, and sitting down and getting up was a slow business.

As she scooped up some more birdseed and scattered it on the paved area beyond the back door she felt the baby move and turn within her. She stilled a moment, letting the movement subside.

Her time was coming…her due date approaching. No longer weeks—only days.

She walked slowly, ponderously, to the sink, filled up the kettle, set it to boil. A cup of tea to while away the time. She could do some sketching—but what for? She'd done a little, from time to time, but had no heart for it. The one of the garden and seascape that she'd made at the hotel in Selcombe had never been finished. She did not want to think about it. Didn't want to think about the time she'd spent there that had ended so disastrously...

She felt a twisting inside her—like ropes pulling tight, into knots.

Isn't this enough of a mess without...?

She tried to pull her thoughts away, as she had been training herself to do ever since she had fled, so urgently, so desperately, to find refuge here in this anonymous little house. Somewhere she could hole up...hide...

But how could she hide? This place, this time, was a respite only. Nothing more than that. Soon—and it was coming ever closer—in a handful of days, she must see Vincenzo again. She might wish with all her being that she need not do so, but how could she deny him?

Impossible to do so.

Her words, hurled at him so long ago now, speared in her head.

'I am handcuffed to you—shackled to you!'

Emotion twisted inside her again. The irony of it was hard to bear.

I didn't want anything to do with him because I loathed him. Now...

She stared blindly out of the kitchen window as the kettle started to boil. Outside the birds pecked hungrily at the seed she'd scattered for them, unseen by her. Emotion came again—a physical pain, stabbing at her. Unbearable to bear—and yet she must. For what else could she do but bear it? What else but endure the ultimate folly she had committed?

Not her pregnancy—not that at all.

A smothered cry of anguish broke from her and she

turned away, hand pressed against her mouth, tears starting in her eyes.

How can I bear it?

But it was beyond answering.

Vincenzo pulled the car against the kerb, turned off the engine. He looked at the small terraced house he'd parked outside in this market town in a popular tourist area of East Anglia. He knew what to expect—he had checked it out online, on the holiday letting agency's website, when Siena had given him her new address. He'd offered to pay for it, but she'd refused. She was refusing all financial support and he had accepted her refusal. As he had accepted everything else…

He felt himself tense. This would not be easy, but it had to be done. Her due date was imminent and he would be here, at her side. Literally so—for he'd rented the house next to hers, also a holiday let, and would stay for the duration. Stay while he could be of use to her.

And then…

No, he would not go there. Not yet.

Impossible to look beyond what was about to happen.

Starting right now.

With a determined movement he got out of the car, walked up to her front door, rapped on it with the knocker. She knew he was coming. He had texted her when he'd set off from London, having flown in the day before. He'd told her his ETA here, then texted again, pulling over on the outskirts of the town, to say he was making his way to her house.

She'd simply texted back:

OK

His mouth pressed. 'OK' was not what it was…

But there was nothing he could do about it. Nothing except what she wanted him to do.

Accept her decision.

The one she'd made all those months ago, when she was fleeing from him…

Siena heard the door knocker, tensing immediately. For a moment she did not move. Then, heavily, she levered herself up and out of the armchair she'd sunk into to watch something mindless on TV. It took her a while to get up—it increasingly did now. Ponderously she made her way out of the living room, down to the front door, steeling herself to open it.

He was standing there, tall against the wintry dusk. She felt her stomach clench, her senses reel from his physical presence after so long a time, but she stood back so he could come inside.

For a moment, though, he was motionless. Siena assumed he was taking in just how very different she looked from when he had last seen her.

'I told you I would look like an elephant by this time,' she said.

She kept her voice neutral, and so was his reply.

'Hardly,' he replied, temporising. 'But you are very near your time now.'

He walked in. The narrow hallway only just let him

pass her. The brush of his sleeve made her stiffen, and as he walked past she caught the distinctive trace of his aftershave. For a second she felt faint with familiarity... with memory.

Memory she must not allow.

Too dangerous.

Too pointless...

Because he is not here for me! He is here only because I am about to give birth to the baby I have conceived. No other reason.

No other reason at all.

And I must have no other reason either! Must allow myself none.

She must match him in the way she was with him now.

'It still could be up to another fortnight,' she said, following him as he stepped into the little sitting room. 'I hope it isn't, though—I just want it over and done with.'

He turned to look at her, his face unreadable.

'How was the drive?' she asked, to take her mind off what it did not help her to think about. 'It's not the easiest part of the world to get to.'

'It was fine,' he said. 'Sat nav did it all.' His eyes were on her still, and still unreadable. 'How have you been keeping, Siena?' he asked.

'OK,' she answered. 'My ankles have swollen a little, but—'

'That's not good!' he cut across her sharply, frowning.

She shook her head, negating his reaction. 'I'm within normal range. No sign of pre-eclampsia. All my readings are fine. I saw the midwife this morning, and she's happy with everything. She said that if I'm not in labour by midweek she'll come again to check on me.'

She didn't want him fussing.

'Can I make you a coffee?' she offered, to stop any more questions. 'This place comes with a coffee machine—though it's probably a bit basic for you. Come into the kitchen and see.'

She led the way, knowing she was waddling, but there was nothing she could do about it. Absently, her hand touched her distended abdomen, as if she were patting a puppy that did not know how much disruption it was causing, but whose feelings she did not want to hurt all the same.

Because it's not your fault, little one. None of this. You couldn't help being conceived the way you were!

'There's a choice of coffee pods,' she said, opening an ornamental tin box beside the coffee machine on the worktop. 'I've used all the decaf ones. And anyway, these days I prefer something that's more easily digestible. I'll make a mint tea for myself.'

She went to fill the kettle, memory filling her head as well. She'd asked for a mint tea at the end of that tasting menu dinner at the seaside hotel and had never drunk it.

She had run instead.

Knowing she had to.

It had been too dangerous…much too dangerous…to do anything but run…

But I ran in vain.

She snapped the memory off. There was no point to it…no purpose.

He was stepping forward to make his selection of coffee pods and Siena moved away. For the first time she was glad of being the size she was. She could not have looked more different than she had that night at the hotel in Devon. Then, pregnancy had given her a bloom, enhancing her looks.

Dangerously so.

Disastrously so.

She pulled her thoughts away again. She must not indulge them. However hard—unbearable—it was to have Vincenzo here now, at this time, she had to endure it. He had a right to be here.

It was not his fault any more than it was her baby's fault that her life was now the mess it was. The mess that was infinitely worse than she had ever thought it would be the day she'd found herself pregnant.

Anguish bit again.

She took a breath as she flicked on the kettle, steadying herself as she often must now.

Vincenzo switched on the coffee machine, turned to look at her. 'I was wondering,' he said, his voice careful, 'if you would like to have dinner with me tonight?'

She shook her head. 'I get very tired now, and I go to bed very early. Do try the pub in the market square for yourself, though. It's supposed to be pretty good—at least by local standards.'

'Thank you—I'll try it out.' His eyes were resting on her, still unreadable. 'And how are *you*, Siena?' he asked. 'Not just physically, but—'

'I'm fine,' she said, cutting across him. There had been concern in his voice, and she did not want that. She could cope with him being here only by keeping well clear of anything personal. 'Like I said,' she went on, 'I'm just keen to get a move on now.'

He nodded in acknowledgement. 'That I can understand,' he said. He paused a moment. Then, 'Do you want to tell me what your birth plan is? I... I would like to be there...or close by...if you will allow me.'

She looked at him uncertainly. 'I... I don't know. If you want to be at the hospital while it's all going on, I guess I don't mind. As for a birth plan... Well, nothing out of the ordinary. I assume I'll want pain relief at some point. Other than that...just as it happens, I suppose. My grab bag's all ready—by my bedroom door. That's it, really.'

The coffee machine finished just as the kettle boiled. She turned off both, making her mint tea while Vincenzo reached forward to take his coffee. An ache filled her. To be here with him, like this, in such circumstances...

Isn't it enough of a mess already? Without me messing it up even more?

Anguish clutched at her again. Why, oh, why had she allowed what was already an impossible situation...one she'd never wanted...to become so much worse?

'Siena?'

Vincenzo's voice made her start. Hastily, she grabbed her mint tea. 'Come into the sitting room,' she said, heading heavily for the kitchen doorway.

'Are you all right? You look...upset.'

Concern was in Vincenzo's voice. It hurt to hear it.

'Just tired,' she said, making her way to the armchair and lowering herself ponderously into it.

'I'll leave you in peace as soon as I've drunk my coffee,' Vincenzo was saying.

She was grateful. This was an ordeal, and it was hard—so very hard.

But I have to get used to seeing him again—to him being around. I have to!

He was sitting himself down on the sofa opposite the armchair, crossing one long leg over the other. She wanted to gaze at him. Gaze at him and drink him in…

But I can't. He isn't mine to gaze at. He's just the man who fathered my baby, and he is concerned only for that reason.

That was all she had to remember.

She took a sip of her mint tea, aware that he was speaking again.

'Is there anything that you might like to do over the weekend?' he asked.

'Not really.'

She didn't mean to sound indifferent, but the weekend was just another two days to get through—two days closer to her due date.

'Well, then, I wondered…' His voice was cautious, speculative, his eyes resting on her with the same careful expression. 'I wondered whether you would feel up to an outing by car? Nothing strenuous. And only if you would like it.' He paused. 'You told me you grew up in this part of the country. Is that why you chose to base yourself here?'

'It seemed as good a reason as any,' she answered. 'I know the district hospital has a good reputation, and I had to settle somewhere—at least for the duration of my being pregnant. What I'll do afterwards I don't yet know…'

Her voice trailed off. She could feel Vincenzo's eyes resting on her, and wished they would not.

'I would still like to help you—' he began.

'No.' Her voice steeled. 'Vincenzo, please—we've had

this discussion. I... I need to make my own way after...
after the baby is born. Deal with it in my own way.'

Deal with so much more than simply having a baby...

She gave a sigh. It was all such a mess. A mess from
beginning to end. Vincenzo had said that it need not
be—but it was.

Longing filled her, intense and hopeless. This whole
situation was wretched—her unwanted pregnancy, her
poor, benighted little baby being born into such a mess,
with neither of its parents welcoming its arrival but seeing it only as a problem, a difficulty...

And now, on top of all of that—

She thrust it from her. What was the point of brooding over it? She had to cope with it—and she had to get
used to coping with having Vincenzo showing up. What
else could she do?

After all he would be doing it for years ahead. Years
she could not bear to think about.

'Maybe,' she heard herself saying now. 'Going for a
drive tomorrow might be OK.'

His expression altered. Lightened fractionally. But it
was still careful.

'If the weather is sufficiently clement, we shall do
so,' he said. 'Would setting off at, say, eleven suit you?
We could drive out somewhere, maybe have lunch, then
circle back? Have a think about where you might like to
go. This part of England is all new to me, so I am happy
to be guided by you.'

He drained the last of his coffee, set the cup aside,
stood up.

'I will leave you in peace now,' he said. 'Settle myself in next door. No, don't get up. I can see myself out.'

'Thank you,' she said, glad she did not have to lumber to her feet.

At the door to the narrow hallway he paused, looking back at her. 'You must phone me,' he said, 'at any time, if you have any need—'

'I'll be fine,' she said.

For a moment longer he let his unreadable gaze rest on her. Then, with a final nod, after bidding her a murmured goodnight, he took his leave.

Leaving her alone.

Alone, alone, alone...

Tears welled in her eyes. Such useless tears...

Vincenzo rapped on Siena's front door. It was a bright, sunny day, promising spring. A good day for a drive in the countryside. He was glad she'd agreed to it. She had not looked very well yesterday, he thought. Not ill, thankfully, but not...not *blooming*.

In her earlier stages, and at the seaside, there had been a radiance to her—a glow playing over her natural, effortless beauty which had been noticeably absent yesterday. Yes, of course her figure had ballooned, this close to full term, but it was more than that. There was an air about her of...not weariness, precisely, but lassitude, perhaps.

He frowned. Depression? He could understand that she was impatient for her due date to arrive, but there had been no eagerness for it.

His face shadowed. Nor could there be for him.

How could there be?

Bleakness filled him. The situation was damnable...

The door opened and Siena was there.

'Ready to set off?' he asked. He forced his voice to sound light.

She nodded. She was wearing a padded but light-weight knee-length coat that emphasised her bulk, but which was presumably warm enough for winter walking. Stout and solid-looking lace-up shoes were on her feet, and she was wearing fleecy trousers. Her hair was bunched back on her head, and her skin looked blotchy.

For a second Vincenzo wanted to ask if she was OK— because it looked as if she had been crying. He started to frown, but he got no chance to say anything, because Siena was talking, constraint in her voice.

'I need to sit on a towel over a polythene bin bag,' she said, and he saw she was holding both items.

'Bin bag...?' Vincenzo stared.

'And a towel, yes. I'm only a handful of days away from my due date.'

Comprehension dawned. 'I'll put them on the seat,' he said, and took them from her.

Settling her in to the passenger seat took some time, but it was done in the end. He helped her draw the seat belt around what once had been her waist. Then, finally arranged, she stretched out her legs and turned towards him.

'Have you had any ideas where you might like to go?'

He could still hear that constraint in her voice, and could see it in the way she sat. Would this outing work at all? He could only try...

'I'm easy,' he said. 'Do you have any preferences?'

'Probably best not to try for the coast but stick to inland.'

She gave directions and Vincenzo followed them. The

flat, arable landscape was very different from that of hilly, pastoral South Devon, but he made no reference to it. Their time there—the way it had ended—lay between them, unspoken of and impossible to mention. Instead, he asked general questions about the area, and Siena politely gave answers, her air of constraint still palpable.

As for him…

Their encounter yesterday had not been easy, but he had not expected it to be. What had been achieved between them—their comfortable companionship during their time in Devon—had gone.

I destroyed it.

And now—now all he could do was what he was doing. Being here to support her in whatever way he could, whatever way she would allow. Ready to take on the responsibility of a parental role he had never looked for but now had to shoulder.

However impossible that might be.

As he drove his eyes slid to her, sitting beside him, her face in profile, her gravid body expectant. Soon—within days—his life would change irrevocably and for ever.

It already has.

But not just because of the baby…

'Shall we find somewhere to stop for lunch soon?'

Siena gave a little start at Vincenzo's voice.

'Yes, good idea,' she said politely.

His question had interrupted her thoughts, which had been drifting, formless and shapeless, as they'd motored on. Though it had brought painful reminders of their time in Devon, it had been soothing, in a way, to drive around like this. She hadn't been anywhere except to the local clinic and for hospital appointments.

Absently, as it so often did, her hand went to the swell of her body, as if with compunction.

Poor little mite. Coming into the world like this...

'What about that place coming up?'

Again, Vincenzo's voice interrupted her thoughts.

She looked to where he was indicating. It looked a decent enough place, typical Suffolk pink, prosperous-looking, with a blackboard sign outside saying *Good Food!* It would do as well as anywhere.

He pulled across to it, driving the car into a small but busy car park—another encouraging indicator. Getting out took a while, and she flexed her legs, feeling elephantine and regretting, for a moment, having come out at all. But they were here now, and she was feeling hungry. Besides, she could do with using the facilities...

Vincenzo guided her inside. Memory pierced of how they'd toured the Devon countryside, explored the Jurassic Coast, how they'd walked along Jane Austen's Cobb, in Lyme, and then tried out the Ammonite Pavement to look for fossils. How that midwife with the jumpy dog had told her to enjoy being pregnant, said how excited she must be feeling, and Vincenzo too, how happy they must be...

How hollow that had sounded, even then.

And now—

It was a thousand times more hollow...

'Will this table suit?'

Vincenzo's polite enquiry interrupted memories that only brought pain.

'Yes, it's fine. I'll join you in a moment.'

She disappeared off in the direction of the washrooms. She felt self-conscious, walking across to them, but there was nothing she could do about that. On her way back to the table a few minutes later she caught a woman seated at another table giving Vincenzo the once-over. He was oblivious to it. As she approached the table the woman saw her, saw how pregnant she was, and looked away, consigning Vincenzo to the category of 'taken'.

But he isn't, is he? And one day—one day when he is simply doing a duty visit to the baby he never asked for, never wanted, would never welcome but only feel responsible for—he will meet a woman who will captivate him, who won't mind that he has a spare son or daughter somewhere in England, by a woman he only ever spent two nights with...

She dragged her thoughts away. Why torment herself with them? To what purpose?

None.

She sat down heavily in the chair Vincenzo had stood to draw back for her, murmuring an awkward thank-you.

If the baby arrives on its due date, then in a couple of weeks' time Vincenzo will be gone. He'll be back in Italy. Back in his own life. And I—

But she didn't want to think about that.

Could not bear to.

Vincenzo finished his beer. His mood was bleak. He and Siena had made stilted conversation over lunch, and now she had disappeared off to the Ladies' again. The rest of the day stretched ahead. And all the days until her time finally came.

Had it been a mistake to turn up like this? Should

he rather have left Siena alone at this time, not insist he be there?

Heaviness weighed him down. The situation was impossible.

And he had made it so.

That night in Devon—

He stamped down his thoughts. They were to no purpose. The situation was as it was.

Damnable.

Memory speared in him—the words Siena had hurled at him all that time ago.

'I am handcuffed to you—shackled to you!'

His eyes lifted from the menu.

Dread filled him at the future looming for him.

But it had to be faced. No escape from it.

His eyes went across the room. Siena was emerging from the Ladies' room, making her way towards him. He got to his feet, holding her chair for her to sit down. There was an odd expression on her face. Puzzled...

'I'm sorry if this is TMI—too much information—but I seem to be bleeding.' She frowned. 'It's not much, but it's definitely blood. I'm not sure what to do. Probably best to ignore it. I'll phone the midwife when we get back. I'm sure she'll just say it happens sometimes and tell me not to worry about it.'

She moved to sit down, but Vincenzo forestalled her. 'I think we ought to go,' he said.

She looked at him. 'Don't you want a pudding?'

He shook his head. 'I'll pay the bill,' he said, picking up the chit.

He crossed to the bar.

'I'd like to pay,' he said.

The barman, who was pulling a pint for another customer, nodded. 'Be right with you.'

'Now,' said Vincenzo.

Whatever he'd put into his voice—and he'd done so quite deliberately—it got results. Moments later Vincenzo was walking back to Siena. She was resting her hand on the back of her chair, as if leaning her weight on it.

He held his arm out to her, and though she hesitated for a moment, she took it. She was soon leaning on him, and frowning slightly.

They left the pub, Vincenzo ushering her into the car deliberately unhurriedly. He helped to settle her, ensuring, as she stipulated, that the towel was thickly folded over the bin bag. Then he got into his side of the car, but did not start the engine immediately. Instead, he keyed a destination into the sat nav.

'What are you doing?' Siena asked beside him.

He turned towards her.

'I'm taking you to hospital,' he said.

CHAPTER TWELVE

'*Hospital?*' Siena's voice was a protest. 'In heaven's name, why? I'm perfectly all right! I haven't got a twinge or anything! Absolutely nothing that might be even the start of a contraction! Not a real one, anyway. I've had the Braxton-Hicks false ones from time to time, but that's perfectly normal.'

He was gunning the engine, heading back on to the road.

'Vincenzo, please! This is quite unnecessary. The hospital will only send me away again! They haven't got room to keep a load of pre-labour women hanging about till their due dates!'

His response was to speed up and throw a glance at her.

'Phone your midwife,' he said.

It was not a suggestion.

Her brow furrowed, but she fished her phone out of her handbag, flicked into her contacts file and hit speed dial. As she waited to connect, she pressed her free hand over her abdomen. A thought struck her, and her frown deepened. When had she last felt any movement?

A moment later her midwife was answering.

And when she hung up, a couple of minutes later, Siena felt fear like ice in her veins…

Vincenzo's grip on the steering wheel was whitening his knuckles. In his head, one word was stabbing:

Damnable.

That was what he'd called the situation. And now, with that single announcement by Siena, the word had been wiped out of existence. Totally overridden.

He dropped his eyes to the sat nav screen. Twenty miles still. Twenty miles to drive as fast and as smoothly as he could. Whether he broke the speed limit or not he neither knew nor cared. If the police stopped them— well, maybe he'd get a blue light escort to the hospital…

He'd glanced at Siena as she hung up from the midwife. Her face had been pale. He'd asked her to put the call on speaker phone, and the midwife had been very good. Not alarmist, but insistent.

'We need to check you out at the hospital,' she'd said. 'Phone again when you are closer.'

What she had not said was what she was going to be checking. But Vincenzo knew perfectly well. What had immediately stabbed in his head—what could be happening…

Placental abruption—the separation of the placenta from the uterine wall…and how dangerous that is…

A knife twisted inside him and his grip on the steering wheel tightened again. More than anyone, he knew that childbirth could be dangerous…

He depressed the accelerator further. 'How are you feeling?' he asked.

He heard her swallow, but she said, 'Fine. I feel fine.

It's just that—' Her voice changed. And he could hear the thread of fear in it now. 'Vincenzo, I can't feel the baby moving—and the towel I'm sitting on feels damp.'

'I'll get you there.' His voice was grim.

The miles passed with punishing resistance, and without the sat nav he'd have been lost. It took them right to the hospital turning. Without wasting time parking, he steered straight to the entrance for the maternity unit, pulled up short. Siena had phoned the midwife again, and was on the phone to her now.

'She says she'll be in the lobby—you should grab a wheelchair. They'll take me straight up.'

Her voice was shaky.

He launched himself out of the driver's seat, hazard lights flashing, saw a row of wheelchairs under a shelter and grabbed one, coming round to Siena's side of the car. She was already opening the door and he helped her out, helped her into the wheelchair, hurried her through the automatically opening doors.

A woman in scrubs was hurrying towards them.

'You made good time—well done.' She nodded at Vincenzo. 'We'll take over now—get your car parked and come on up. You can be there for the examination—we don't know what's happening yet.'

Then she turned her attention to Siena and pushed her across the lobby, clearly hurrying.

Vincenzo went back out to the car, slamming the passenger door shut, throwing himself in on his side His glance went to where she'd been sitting. The towel on the seat was pale grey—except for the large bloodstain in the centre...

He felt sick suddenly. But not because of the blood...

Less than five minutes later he'd disposed of the car and was back inside the maternity unit lobby, pushing through the doors where Siena had disappeared.

A medic of some sort walked past him, and he grabbed his arm. 'Possible placental abruption—where would she be taken?' His voice was urgent.

The medic turned. 'Follow me.'

Siena heard the words, but scarcely comprehended them. Yet they were clear enough.

Emergency Caesarean.

She stared, white-faced, heart thudding, the ice in her veins colder still, at the consultant obstetrician, summoned by the midwife, who'd said those words to her.

'It has to be now. Right now,' he said.

His voice was calm, but insistent.

The door to the examination room swung open and Vincenzo was there, striding in.

'Vincenzo!' she cried.

He came to her at once, lying there on the examination couch. She was aware she was hardly in any state for him to see her, but she didn't care. All she cared about was what the obstetrician had just announced.

Vincenzo took her outstretched hand, squeezed it. Turned to the obstetrician.

'It has to be a C-section delivery straight away,' the consultant told him gravely. 'The placenta is coming away and the baby is becoming increasingly at risk. Hypoxia is—'

'Yes, I know.' Siena heard Vincenzo's voice cut across him, sounding not curt, but short. 'Potentially—'

He didn't complete the sentence, and Siena gave a terrified moan. Her free hand flew to her abdomen. As if her bare, splayed hand could keep her baby safe. Alive...

The baby she had never welcomed...

Her eyes flew to the obstetrician.

'Do it!' she cried. 'Just do it now! Do whatever it takes!'

The consultant nodded, and she saw his glance go to Vincenzo.

'I want him with me!' she cried, and clung to his hand in desperation.

'Of course,' said the consultant. He turned to the hovering midwife. 'Theatre One,' he said. 'Let's go.'

After that it was a blur. A blur that was a nightmare. She felt herself being slid sideways onto a trolley and wheeled off. Her hand still clung to Vincenzo's, as he kept pace with the trolley, and it was all that kept her going...all that she could hold on to in an ocean of terror.

So much more than terror.

Emotions poured through her like a tsunami sweeping her up, convulsing her, buckling her into a tiny piece of flotsam torn apart by the power of what was ripping her to pieces. Words flew through her head—fragments, shreds, rags and tatters—each one suffocating her with its terrifying intensity.

I never wanted this baby. I was resentful and resistant—appalled and self-pitying—angry at its conception. A self-indulgent, irresponsible conception, by self-indulgent, irresponsible parents. All I cared about was that my life was being changed for ever, that I was sacrific-

*ing my dream of art college again. I never wanted this
baby...my poor baby...*

And now...

Terror constricted her again and she could barely
breathe.

The medics seemed to be crowding round her, talking over her, talking to her only to tell her what was es-
sential. Not one of them was telling her the only thing
she was desperate to know.

Is it too late?

But she couldn't ask—and knew they wouldn't tell
her anyway. Her grip on Vincenzo's hand tightened. He
was saying nothing—not to her, not to the doctors. She
knew she had to let the doctors get on with it.

Silently, terrified, she urged them on.

Hurry—hurry—hurry!

She was being put into some kind of hospital gown,
then turned on her side. Vincenzo was still holding her
hand, and some kind of injection was being made into
her spine. Then some kind of screen was being placed
below her ribs and she couldn't see anything—anything
at all—or feel anything except the tsunami of terror, of
guilt, churning her into pieces...

Her other hand, which could no longer go to where it
longed to be, started to flail helplessly, hopelessly, and
Vincenzo caught it, pressed it with his own.

'Stay calm...they are doing what they must.'

His voice was strained, his expression strained too,
and her eyes clung to his. There was desperation in her
clinging. Despair in her terrified, whispering voice.

'We're losing our baby—oh, Vincenzo, we're losing
our baby!'

Nothing else mattered. Nothing at all...

Only the fear, the terror, knifing her over and over again...

He pressed her hands, saying nothing—because what, she thought fearfully, could he say?

What was going on beyond the screen she did not know—dared not know. Knew only that it was taking an unbearably, agonisingly long time.

Until...

There was movement. Something was happening. Though she could still feel nothing...nothing at all. To the side of the screen she could see the midwife carrying something...something that made no noise.

She gave a broken cry, and Vincenzo twisted to see what he could, never letting go of her hands, which he was crushing with his own.

'What is it? What's happening?' Her voice was anguished.

But she knew. She knew what was happening...what had happened. Knew it because she deserved it... Knew it because suddenly the obstetrician was there, looking down at her. He was about to tell her, *I'm so sorry. We did all we could, but it was too late...*

Grief convulsed her, possessed her.

And then...

A cry...a thin, frail cry. A baby's cry...a cry of life...

'You have a little boy,' the consultant said. 'Congratulations.'

Another cry broke the air. Not a baby's cry—her own. Her face convulsed again, tears suddenly pouring from her eyes, blurring her vision completely.

And then she heard another voice. Vincenzo's.

Low, and deep, and wrung with emotion.

'Dio sia ringraziato,' he said.

God be thanked.

Vincenzo shut his eyes.

God be thanked.

It rang in his head, again and again. Relief such as he had never known knifed through him. Then he realised the consultant was speaking again, and made himself open his eyes, listen to what was being said.

The obstetrician was addressing Siena, but he threw an encouraging smile at Vincenzo as well. 'Now, I'm just going to finish off…tidy up. Then I'll zip you back up, make sure everything's tucked away neatly,' he went on, 'and then we'll get you into Recovery. But first…'

He turned away, beckoned to the midwife who was just scooping something up. She came towards them. A little mewing sound came from the white-wrapped bundle in her arms. The obstetrician disappeared behind his screen again.

'Here he is,' said the midwife.

And she placed into Siena's outstretching arms the most perfect human being who had ever existed…

Siena gazed and gazed as love—instant, overwhelming, overpowering love—poured through her.

'Oh, my darling…my darling one…my darling…'

The tiny, perfect face of her tiny, perfect baby looked up at her. And her love for him encompassed her, became her whole being for ever and for ever.

Then another voice was speaking, low and impassioned. *'Lui è perfetto. Perfetto! Il nostro piu prezioso—'*

Siena's hand pressed his arm. 'Our son,' she said. 'Oh, Vincenzo…'

He crouched down beside her, his eyes only for the tiny, so precious bundle in her arms. Tears stood in his eyes.

'I never realised—' he said.

She looked at him. 'Nor I…'

Then the midwife was speaking, smiling down at them both. 'He's doing very well, considering. I'm sorry it was all so dramatic, but these things can happen. We're going to pop him into Neonatal ICU, just to—'

Siena's eyes flew up, a cry breaking from her. *'ICU?'* Stark terror was in her voice suddenly.

'For observation only…just for a little while,' the midwife was instantly reassuring.

'There's something wrong!'

The terror was still in Siena's voice. Her eyes distended. Fear hollowing her out.

Something wrong! I knew there would be…that I couldn't…that I didn't deserve…

The midwife was speaking again, calmly and clearly. 'No, there is nothing wrong. I promise you. All the signs are good. We just want to ensure he gets a really good start after his rushed arrival.'

She felt Vincenzo's hand tighten on her shoulder. 'So there is nothing to fear?' he asked.

Siena could hear the same note of terror in his voice as had been in hers. Her hand clutched his sleeve.

'Nothing at all,' the midwife said firmly.

'Exactly so!' The voice of the obstetrician, busy behind his screen, corroborated the midwife's assurance.

Siena felt the terror draining away, felt Vincenzo's hand lighten on her shoulder.

She heard the midwife continue, brightly, 'So, enjoy this time with him, both of you, and then we can get all of you out of Theatre.'

She smiled benignly, then disappeared behind the screen again, where whatever was being done to her Siena could not feel, and right now did not want to know. Because all that existed in the entire world was what was here—for which she was so grateful…so abjectly, desperately, heart-wrenchingly grateful.

The precious, perfect baby in her arms.

Vincenzo stood by his parked hire car, still dazed. When he'd parked the car in daylight, all those hours ago, all that had been in him was the urgency that had possessed him since they'd begun heading to the hospital, the knifing fear he'd been trying to hide from Siena, because it would only add to hers. Now, the entire universe was transformed.

Slowly, he opened the car door, got into the driving seat. He felt overwhelmed, wrung out. And at the same time…

He closed his eyes a moment, feeling the emotion that had possessed him ever since that first frail cry had told him that his desperate prayers had been answered possess him again, more strongly yet. Gratitude, thankfulness pierced him. And more.

Remorse.

I didn't realise—I didn't know.

But now he did. And it was a gift past counting.

The same words that had broken from him as he'd

heard that thin cry, heard the obstetrician speak, were searing in his head again.

God be thanked.

His eyes opened, he turned the key in the ignition, reversed the car out of its parking space. He would return to the house next to Siena's. In the morning he would come to the hospital again, bringing her bag with him. She would need to be in hospital for a few days, but he'd asked for her to be moved to a private room when it was medically safe. As for his son...

My son!

The words rang in his head. Such incredible, wonderful words—so infinitely precious.

He'd been able to see him, cocooned in his neonatal protection, fast asleep, ignorant of all the monitoring of his vital functions. He'd reported back to Siena, repeating all the medical reassurances given him, and what they had already been told—that his stay there should not be long, and that on the morrow she could have him with her.

'Now, you get some sleep. Rest and recover.' He'd smiled down at her, then left.

She'd looked exhausted...

Emotion twisted inside him. He set it aside.

Drove away from the hospital.

CHAPTER THIRTEEN

THE PRIVATE ROOM was very comfortable, and Siena sat, propped up with pillows behind her back, gazing down at her baby son in his hospital crib beside her. Fast, fast asleep—and so, so tiny.

And safely out of ICU—blessedly.

He was completely safe. That was what the consultant had assured her when he'd called by this morning.

'His arrival was dramatic, but he has taken no harm from it…none at all. All his vital signs are totally normal,' he had told her.

'Are you sure? Are you absolutely sure?' Siena's voice had been fearful.

'Absolutely. He is completely healthy. No cause for any concern at all.'

She clung to the words now, as she gazed into the crib. Emotions flowed through her—a tangled, overpowering mix. So much emotion…for so many reasons…

A nurse tapped on the door, put her head around it. 'You have a visitor,' she said brightly.

Vincenzo walked in.

Siena felt something leap inside her—hold for a moment. Then it subsided. She made it subside.

He looked at her, but only briefly, as if in greeting,

and then his eyes dropped to the crib, his expression changing. As if reluctant to look away, he looked quickly back at Siena. This time he smiled. But it was a careful smile, she could see.

'How are you?' he asked.

The concern in his voice was real, though, and she appreciated it. Appreciated it so much. Emotion turned over inside her.

'Fine,' she said. 'I'm on painkillers, and will be for a while. But they've made me walk about a bit already— they say it's good for me.' She glanced across at the crib. 'And, as you can see, he's out of ICU.'

Her voice had softened, relief open in it. She looked back at Vincenzo. So much was inside her, and to some of it she must give voice.

'Oh, dear God, Vincenzo...' Her voice was low, heart-felt. 'Thank God you realised what danger I was in—' She broke off, lifted a hand, then let it fall on the bed-clothes again. 'I'd been trying not to look up every single thing that might make me alarmed unnecessarily! I thought it would just work me up into a bag of nerves! The midwife had said everything was fine, so I was determined not to let myself worry.'

'What happened could not have been predicted,' Vincenzo said. Concern was in his voice.

'But if you hadn't been there—' Fear was in her again.

Vincenzo held up a hand. 'You would have phoned, and your midwife would have called you in—just as happened. You would have taken a taxi to the hospital—you said you had the number on standby. So please do not think about it any more. Everything was safe in the end.'

His gaze went from her back to the crib. 'How is he? He looks so peaceful. So—'

He broke off. Siena could hear the emotion in his voice, see it in his face.

'Perfect,' she said, her own voice softening, filling with love. 'Just perfect.'

For a moment they just gazed at him, so tiny, so perfect...

'Have...have you thought about names?' she heard Vincenzo ask. His voice was tentative.

So was hers as she answered. 'How about something for your father?' she ventured uncertainly.

'My father's name was Roberto,' he said slowly, as if trying it out.

She thought about it, tried it out too. 'Robert in English. Rob or Bob—or Bobby.'

It sounded good.

'And for your father? A second name?' Vincenzo was asking.

The shake of her head was instinctive.

Vincenzo frowned. Looked at her. His gaze searching. Perceptive. 'What is it?'

She didn't answer immediately—could not. Memory was knifing through her—and all the terrible emotions that went with that memory.

She heard Vincenzo draw a chair close, sit down beside her.

'What is it?' he asked again, his voice low. Troubled.

She plucked at her bedclothes, not wanting to look at him. Keeping her gaze lowered. Feeling the overpowering presence of the baby in his crib beside her bed. Her safe, healthy baby...

So utterly unlike—

'Can you tell me?' Vincenzo's voice was still low.

Her face worked. She didn't want to tell him, but knew she must.

There was so much she could not say to him—could never say—but this she could. And maybe she needed to say it for herself, too. To help her make sense of the way she had been since learning she was pregnant.

She took a breath, making herself look at Vincenzo. That itself was hard to do. Emotion twisted inside her— so much emotion—for so many reasons, so tangled and knotted.

But this was one she could unknot...make sense of.

'You asked me when we were in Selcombe why I hadn't gone to art school when I was a teenager.' She began, her voice low. 'I... I never really answered you.'

She paused again, looking away for a moment. Then made herself continue. It was so sorry a tale—so desperately sad...

'I didn't go,' she said, 'because my brother and his wife had just had a baby. And the baby—' She broke off again, then made herself look at Vincenzo, her expression bleak—for what else could it be? 'He was severely disabled,' she said heavily. 'There was a cruel, incurable congenital condition, inherited from my sister-in-law, that meant he was life-limited. He needed round-the-clock support, even when they could finally take him home. They were in pieces...distraught. And I...well, I stayed at home to help them. Practical care, emotional support... It was just...just dreadful.'

She paused again, then made herself continue.

'He was named after my father—and he...he died

last year.' She swallowed painfully. 'His death, expected though it was, broke my brother and his wife. They… they emigrated to Australia, to put it all behind them.'

She broke off, unable to speak any more. Yet there was more that she must say.

'When they moved to Australia,' she said, 'I reapplied to art college, and was accepted again as a mature student. I thought my life—on hold for so long—was finally starting. Until—'

She stopped again. Looked at Vincenzo, sitting beside her, his face sombre.

'I realise now,' she said slowly, 'that what happened to my nephew—which I never wanted to tell you about, or even think about, because it seemed like a dark, frightening shadow over my own pregnancy—affected my reaction to finding myself pregnant. Part of me felt guilty, I suppose, that I was having a baby and my poor brother and sister-in-law had just lost their child. And part of what I felt…' her voice caught '…was…was fear. Yes, I know that my nephew's condition was genetic, that he so tragically inherited it from his mother's side, not my brother's. But still I felt, I suppose, a kind of dread— even though I wouldn't admit it, even though I was having a healthy pregnancy—lest something went wrong for me, too.'

She took a breath, like a knife into her lungs.

'And it so nearly, nearly did!'

She reached for Vincenzo's hand, clutching at it.

'I know… I know you say that even if you hadn't realised how dangerous that bleed was, my midwife would still have called me in, and the outcome would have been

blessedly the same, but it was *you* who saw the danger—'
She broke off again. Then, '*You* saw it! *You* knew it!'

And now it was Vincenzo's turn to speak. Heavily, sombrely. 'There was a reason for that. As your time approached, I ensured I had learnt as much as I could about late pregnancy and labour. What risks might present themselves... What might go wrong.' He stopped. Then: 'You see, I knew things could. Knew things could go wrong. Because...' He took an incising breath. 'Because it did go wrong for my mother. She died.'

Siena could hear the hollowing in his voice.

'She died from complications in labour, giving birth to my still-born sister.'

She saw his eyes go away from her, out across the room, out into the past, to the mother he had lost, the sister he had never known, the father bereft of his wife and daughter. Then they came back to her.

'It was the last thing I wanted to tell you,' he said. 'And maybe...' he took a narrowed breath, '...knowing how my mother's death devastated my father, taking my sister as well, I felt anger somewhere inside...that...that we were having a baby so...so...'

'So carelessly.'

Siena's voice was flat. She held Vincenzo's gaze. Would not flinch from it.

'Both you and I,' she said, 'have tragedy in our families. Loss that should never have been. Not just our parents. Two children...loved and wanted and yet lost. While we—'

She broke off again. Her face buckled, her voice choking now. Emotion overwhelming her. So much emotion. Carried for so long. For nine long months. Suppressed, denied…feared. And now it was pouring through her in an unstoppable tide.

'To think I never wanted to be pregnant! Could only feel how wrong it was! So completely wrong! And then yesterday—oh, dear God, we nearly lost him! We nearly *lost* him!'

She felt the remembered terror of that breakneck drive to the hospital, the horror of realising what was happening—realising, like a blow, just how desperately she wanted this baby, how terrified she was of losing it…

Suddenly she was starting to shake. Tears began to convulse her. She couldn't talk—not any more—as sobs ravaged her. And she was shaking…shaking so much—

And then arms were coming around her. Arms that were strong and sure, folding her against him, holding her, holding her safe while sobs choked in her throat. He was speaking to her, but it was in Italian, so she couldn't understand. And yet she heard the passion in it, the vehemence. Her tears poured and poured until there were no more, and still he held her, gently now, soothing her, his hands warm and safe and protective.

For a long time he went on holding her as her tears ebbed, and it was the only place in all the universe that she wanted to be.

The only place she should not be…

She drew back. 'I'm sorry,' she said chokingly, tearily. 'I know I shouldn't…shouldn't cry. It's just that—' She broke off, unable to say more.

Her hands were still in his, and she was clinging to them, warm and strong. But they were not hers to cling to…

He pressed her fingers. 'There is no more need for

fear,' he said. 'He is well and safe, our Baby Roberto. We can give thanks for that.' He took a breath—a scything one. 'That is all we must think of now. That—and the future.'

Something had changed in his voice...something that made Siena look at him. Her heart was still beating hectically, in the aftermath of her outburst. She felt a chill go through her. Nervelessly, she slipped her fingers from his.

She took a breath. A hard one. A difficult one. Infinitely hard. But one she must take all the same so she could say what she must.

For his sake.

'Vincenzo—it's all right. You...you don't have to say anything. I... I know what the future must be. I've always known.'

She could hear the hollow note in her voice...knew why it was there, knew that it echoed the hollow forming inside her. She made herself go on, knowing she wanted to say it herself, not wait to hear him say it to her. Say what she knew she must.

The tragedy that had so nearly consumed them yesterday had ripped from her all that had meshed about her during her pregnancy: her fears and her guilt, her resentment and her resistance. Ripped them from her and transformed them into what had been so blessedly bestowed upon her—her precious baby son, alive and well and loved with all her heart.

But now she must face what remained to be faced.

For a moment pain lanced in her...and anguish. But she must go on. Because nothing had changed. All the drama and terror of yesterday—it altered nothing.

'I know that now we have to move on,' she said, making herself face him…face what had to be said. 'Move forward. You've been so good,' she went on, 'supporting me as you have. And yesterday…*thank you*…'

She felt her voice become unsteady, forced herself to make it sound more normal, less strained. She must not burden him with her pain, her anguish.

'And thank you now…for coming in, for the private room, for seeing me through to this point. Thank you for all your support! But now…' She swallowed. There seemed to be a stone in her throat, blocking it, making it hard to speak, but speak she must. To say what must be said, cost her what it would. 'Now I don't want…don't want to impose on you any longer—'

'Impose?' There was an edge in his voice suddenly. He pushed back the chair, getting to his feet. Looking down at her, his face shuttered.

She forced herself on. 'You have been so good to me—and yesterday…' She didn't finish—couldn't. Instead she went on: 'I am so, so appreciative. But now you will want to get your own life back.'

He cut across her. 'My own life—?' His voice was flat.

She spoke on, saying the difficult things that had to be said. Even now, after all the trauma, they had to be said. The abject relief of their baby's safe arrival could not last for ever. It had drawn them together in urgency, but now the reality of their situation must apply again. However guilty she felt now, for having come so terrifyingly close to losing her baby, guilty for how she had not welcomed becoming pregnant, had wished it had never happened, that did not blot out all that she must face.

She looked him square in the eyes—but her fingers were working on the folds of her sheet.

'I forced this on you, Vincenzo. Forced on you the knowledge of what had happened that night we spent together. And I know... I know you are grateful for our baby's safe birth, when it might have gone so dreadfully the other way, but I don't want... I don't want that to... to change anything. I mean, I don't want you feeling... obliged...in any way because of that.' She took a breath, made herself go on. 'I know you will always honour what you feel are your responsibilities, but...'

His expression had changed. She had seen it before, that expression—but not for a long, long time.

'Responsibilities? Obligation? Is that what you would reduce me to?'

There was a chill in his voice that reached into her veins. She stared at him, consternation in her face.

'Vincenzo...' Her voice was anguished, each word forced from her, halting and hesitant, but they had to be said—they *had* to. 'We know—we *both* know—that had yesterday been the tragedy it might have been, we...we would never have seen each other again. For there would have been no reason... And I know...' each word was a blade, cutting into her '...that...that our baby is all there is between us—nothing else.'

He was looking at her, and it was unbearable that he should do so. But she must bear it—she must. Even if it was a weight that was crushing her, stifling her...

He was silhouetted against the window, motionless and rigid.

'But that is not true.'

His words fell into the space between them.

* * *

His face was shuttered. His own words echoed in his head.

'But that is not true.'

Not true.

His eyes went to the crib on the other side of her bed. He felt his heart catch, turn over in his chest. His son...

And Siena's too.

But other words overwrote those.

Ours—our son.

Conceived on a night that was impossible to forget. That burned in him still. A night he had since seized a second time—taking her into his arms, into his passionate embrace...

The bitter irony of it tore him like a wolf at his throat.

That first night together it had been he who had left her in the morning, not wanting to face the truth about what had burned so fiercely between them. But that second night...

She left me. And, yes, I have had to respect her wishes, her decision. Had to let her be.

But now...

Now urgency filled him—impelling him to speak.

'That is not true,' he said again.

That morning—that first morning—waking with her... walking out on her. But if I hadn't? If I had stayed? And that second morning—if she had not left...?

But he knew the answer to that question. Knew it because he gave it now.

'Not true,' he said, 'because from the very first there has been something between us.' He paused. 'And there still is, Siena.'

* * *

Her eyes lifted to his, and in his she saw an intensity that stilled her.

'From the very first,' he said again. 'It has been there. And you cannot deny it, Siena—and no more can I. Neither of us. You cannot deny that first night we spent together—'

'It should never have happened!' The cry broke from her.

'Why?' he challenged. 'Because you became pregnant? That does not negate what brought us together that night!' His voice changed. 'And nor does it negate that night in Devon.'

He held up a hand, as if to silence her—but she could not speak, not a word. Tumult was in her. This should not be happening. He should be accepting what she'd said, that there was nothing between them except the baby now sleeping, unconscious of the tormented circumstances of his conception and his birth.

Vincenzo was speaking still, his voice grave, guarded, as if he were picking his words carefully, deliberately.

'When you left that morning in Devon I respected your decision to do so,' he was saying. 'Respected that it signalled—could only signal—that you wanted nothing more to do with me. That for you there was nothing between us other than a pregnancy you had never wanted.'

'But there *was* nothing else! I've said that—known that—all along!' Siena's voice rang out.

'And I tell you that is not true,' Vincenzo said.

Something worked in his face as he stood there, his expression grave, looking down at her. His voice had changed—she didn't know how, or why. Didn't know why there seemed to be something in her throat. Something making it tight.

He was still looking at her. Speaking again. But all the while her throat was tightening yet more. As if to hold something back—something she dared not allow.

'What is it between us, Siena, that draws us together?' he asked.

There was an intensity in his voice now, beneath the gravity, and his eyes were still holding hers, not letting her go... She could see tension in his face, in the stance of his tall body. Felt her own face and body tense in return. Her throat was narrowing still more, making it hard to breathe, and in her chest she could feel her heart thudding.

She heard him answer the question he had just put to her—for she was incapable of answering it...incapable of saying anything...

'The child we created between us? Yes—but how did his conception come to be? It came, Siena, because when I first set eyes on you I wanted you, desired you. In an instant—a second! Overwhelmingly and absolutely. And it was the same for you. That night we spent together proves that beyond all question! And despite everything else that has happened since that night, that desire—that overpowering, overwhelming desire that burnt between us—has been there. And neither of us can deny it!'

He reached for her hands, holding them fast. His expression was no longer grave, but his eyes were still holding hers, not letting go...

'Desire, Siena—that is what draws us together. And has from the very first! In London and, yes, in Devon too—because why else should we have ended back together again as we did? Throwing all our caution to the winds! And there is more...oh, so much more that draws us together! Now we have the miracle of parenthood, so long resisted but now—oh, dear God—treasured and rejoiced in, as it should have been from the first, given to us as a gift beyond measure!'

His voice was shaken, intense—vehement. She could scarcely bear to hear it.

But he was not done yet.

He stood there, beside her hospital bed, so tall, his eyes never letting hers go, and she was helpless—just helpless to do anything but hear his words, feel the constriction of her throat, the thudding of her heart, the catch of her breath in her lungs.

How could she deny what he was telling her? Impossible.

And he was talking still, his eyes still holding hers... just as his hands, so warm, so strong, were holding hers...

'And there is one more thing that can draw us together, bind us, hold us.' His voice changed, softened. 'If we let it.'

She couldn't speak—could only sit there, eyes fastened on his. Her heart now thudding in her chest... ringing in her ears.

'And if you want it,' he said. 'That second night with you told me something—blazed it to me!—that I know now I can never deny. And even if you deny it, or do not feel it—which, if it is so, I must accept, cost me what it will—it changes nothing. Not for me.'

His eyes were pouring into hers, and she was reeling from what was in them. The drumming in her ears was making her feel faint…or something was. But she must speak. She *must*. No matter what it cost her to say it. To dare to say it…

'But for me,' she said, and her voice was so low it was almost a whisper, 'it did change everything. Oh, Vincenzo, what is this "one more thing" that might be between us?'

Anguish was in her eyes, in her face, as she asked him. Asked him the question she could now dare to ask him—risking all.

He gave a slow, grave smile. Lifting his strained features. Transforming them.

'You know its name, Siena, and so do I. So say it.'

But she could not. Could not speak at all. Could only let her hands cling to his, her heart thudding in her chest like a hammer.

'Then I will say it for you,' he said. 'It's the missing piece. We started with desire—instant, blazing and consuming—so strong, so powerful, that we both did something we had never done before to consummate it. And then we jumped straight to parenthood. But we missed out the bit in the middle—the bit that binds the one to the other. I thought… I thought we had had found it, that night in Devon, but—' He broke off, his voice twisting. 'When I woke to find you gone—'

Words burst from her.

'Vincenzo, it's why I fled from you! I couldn't bear it—couldn't bear the realisation! Couldn't bear that it might mean as little to you as our first night together!'

A rasp broke from him—remorse and self-castigation.

'That first night was just desire! Because I would not let it have a chance to be anything more! I feared it—I admit that now. It was only when we had to spend time with each other, because of what that first night had created, that it started to grow. So slowly at first... And then—'

He lifted her hands, clasped them in his, raising first one to his lips and then the other.

'But on our second night... *Then* I knew—oh, I *knew*—' He took a breath—a ragged one. 'I knew, Siena, that I had come to feel for you so much more than mere desire.'

He paused, her hands pressed in his, his eyes pouring into hers. And they were telling her what he now said in words, his voice softening, catching.

'Love, Siena—that is the missing piece. Love that leads from desire to what we have now. Binding the one to the other, bringing us together, now and for ever.' His gaze went to the crib at her side. 'With our son. Our precious, beloved son...'

Tears were sliding down her cheeks. Tears that spoke of so much. Of love given—with anguish in her heart—as she fled his bed after that night in Devon. When she had known that she had fallen in love with him...when she had known that to him she was only a woman of fleeting desire and unwilling parenthood.

Her tears were for hopeless love, and the anguish of her months away from him, alone and pregnant, knowing that for all her days, the rest of her life, she must share the child she had conceived with a man who would only ever desire her...and nothing more.

And now she felt her heart blossom and flower, and sweet, sweet air fill her lungs, dissolving the unbearable ache in her throat. And now her fears, her anguish, had vanished, were no more, and never again would be. For now the love she had thought only she felt was his too—for her. Love given and returned...

She said his name haltingly, through the tears sliding down her cheeks. He lowered himself beside her, leaning over her to kiss them away softly, gently, tenderly.

Lovingly.

'No more tears, Siena,' he said, kissing the last away.

'It's my hormones,' she said, and her voice held a shaky laugh through the tears.

'And love, Siena. Love—what else?'

Through the mist of her tears she saw his eyes were moist, as they had been when their precious son had been placed in her arms.

She gave a choke, words falling from her. 'I left you that morning in Devon because I could not bear that after such a night you would think it a mistake...regret it as you did our first night! I could bear it that first time, but not again—not when I awoke in your arms and knew that I was in love with you. And that is why...why I have kept away from you...kept you away! Because I could not bear to know that at best you would never want from me anything more than desire, and at worst...not even that. All these months without you have been agony—agony because I knew that I had fallen in love with you, and that for the rest of my life it would be a torment to have you being the father of my baby but never anything more!'

'And that is what I thought I faced too!' His voice was rough with emotion. 'These last hellish months, with you keeping me at bay, when all I wanted in the world was to come to you, be with you, stay with you—' He broke off, taking a ragged, razored breath. 'Damnable! That's what it's been! Damnable to know that I loved you and

you could not bear me near you. Damnable to think that I
would have to face all the years ahead, sharing with you
our son—but nothing else! Damnable to think that one
day you would find someone to love of your own, and I
would have to stand aside and let it happen! Damnable!'

A sob broke from her. 'Oh, Vincenzo—what fools
we've been! What *fools*!'

She gave another choking cry and held him closer to
her yet, her lips pressed against his. Emotion was pouring through her, filling her to the brim, overflowing...

So much emotion. And with one name—only one.

Love.

He had said it, declared it, and she had too. So what
use was it for her to try and deny it still—to deny what
he had said?

None.

And never again would there be denial. *Never.*

She clung to him as he kissed her, possessively, cherishingly, and she kissed him back, just as possessively,
as cherishingly. Tears sprang in her eyes...tears of diamonds, of rainbows...

He drew back a little, but only to lift his mouth from
hers and smile at her, looking deep into her eyes. She
said his name, low and loving, and for a long and timeless moment he simply held her, his gaze pouring into
hers. Then his eyes slipped from her, going to the crib
beyond the bed. Their son slept still, oblivious to all that
was taking place around him. She saw Vincenzo's expression soften. Saw the lovelight in his eyes for her and
for their precious son, loved and adored by them both.

'He brought us together by his conception—and now
he brings us together by his birth,' he said.

'And now,' Siena said softly, her gaze aglow with all the love filling it, filling her whole being, lifting her into a joy she had never known or thought possible, 'we will stay together as he grows, and be there for him all our days.'

She leant back against her pillows, taking Vincenzo's hand, holding it fast. So infinitely much was filling her.

She gazed at him.

The man she loved.

The man she had desired, then hated, then, oh, so slowly come to feel love for—then fled from in fear of those very feelings. And now... Oh, now...

'Is it possible to feel happier?' she asked.

He shook his head. 'No,' he said. 'Unless...' His eyes held hers. 'Siena, I once, in my arrogance, said we should marry.' His voice was rueful, eyes glinting. 'Now,' he said, 'I simply ask you. Be my wife, Siena. Take me for your husband so that the only day we will be happier than we are right now will be on our wedding day.'

She gave a laugh of joy, of love, of a happiness that stretched into the infinity around them. And as she did so another sound came. A tiny mewing sound.

Their eyes flew to the crib.

Their son was waking.

Carefully coming around the bed, Vincenzo lifted him up to place him into her arms.

This token of their love for each other.

This living symbol of their love.

The cause of their love for each other.

For without him...

Thankfulness poured through her as she put her precious infant son—*their* precious infant son—to her breast.

Her joy was complete.

And gently...so gently... Vincenzo—the man she loved, with whom she had made the long, strange, difficult and tormented journey to where they now were and aways would be—brushed his mouth on her forehead as she nursed their newborn son. The reason and the proof and the future of their love.

EPILOGUE

SIENA STOOD IN the quiet churchyard, her hand resting on the arm of the man beside her. They both stood looking down at a tiny grave, its little white headstone nestling between two other graves.

Tears choked her voice as she spoke. 'Thank you... *thank* you for coming,' she said. 'It means so much to me.'

The man beside her pressed the hand on his sleeve with his own hand. 'And to me, too. I am glad to be here.' He paused a moment, his eyes going back to the little white headstone. 'He's safe here, isn't he? With his grandparents. And that is the way I shall think of him and remember him—here, at peace, out of pain and illness. Knowing that you and his new cousin will keep watch over him. And knowing that he will have a brother, soon, who will live to be strong and healthy and with a full term of life.'

Siena heard the emotion rich in her brother's voice and lifted her face to his.

'I am glad more than I can say that you'll be parents again, and that genetic counselling means a healthy baby this time.' She gave a smile. 'When they are both older, the cousins, we'll come and visit you in Australia, I promise. As soon as Bobby's big enough to cope with such a long flight!'

'Try him out on short-haul first—to Italy,' her brother said smilingly. 'I'm glad you're happy about living in Milan,' he added. 'And that you're definitely going to be picking up your art studies in Italy—it's the ideal place for it, after all.' He patted her hand again. 'You're going to Siena for your honeymoon, Vincenzo tells me. Lots of art there—and all with your name on it!'

She nodded. 'It seemed the perfect place to go.'

'Well, then, let's get you married, sis. Come on—time for me to walk you down the aisle.'

They moved away, towards the church familiar to them both from childhood. The three graves marked sadness—but today there was only gladness. It would be a small wedding—just her brother, to give her away, and Megan as maid of honour—and to hold Bobby during the service—enraptured that so happy an ending had come about after such a storm.

They reached the church door.

'Ready, sis?' her brother asked.

The strains of the ancient organ struck up.

'Ready,' affirmed Siena.

They stepped through and Siena's eyes went, like a homing arrow, to the man standing by the altar rail.

Vincenzo. The man she loved with all her heart and soul and being.

He turned his head to smile at her. And in that smile was all the love he held for her and always would.

The organ swelled and on her brother's arm Siena walked beside him. To marry the beloved father of their beloved son and be his wife—his beloved wife—for all eternity.

* * * * *

HARLEQUIN
Reader Service

Enjoyed your book?

Try the perfect subscription for Romance readers and get more great books like this delivered right to your door.

See why over 10+ million readers have tried Harlequin Reader Service.

Start with a Free Welcome Collection with free books and a gift—valued over $20.

Choose any series in print or ebook.
See website for details and order today:

TryReaderService.com/subscriptions